About The Author

Dan Beeston has been described as a male caucasian, approximately six foot, wearing blue jeans and a dark hoodie, last seen travelling north on foot. He is responsible for hundreds and hundreds of comic strips ranging from poorly judged to exquisitely crafted many of which can be found at invisiblespiders.com

He has been telling stories for most of his adult life but this is the first time he's put one this long into a big paper-filled rectangle.

EVERYTHING YOU EVER WANTED

Dan Beeston

For Steve,
Steve
and heck…
all the Steves

Prologue

Most people are quite average. Indeed this is how average is defined. Oh yes each *person* has a thing they are good at. But even most people who are good at a particular thing are average at all of their things in total. And even when compared to all the people who are good at their thing, most people are average. This is mathematics.

It is generally considered quite rude to point this out and it raises the chances of getting a smack in the mouth. This is also mathematics, but a more robust mathematics that is rarely learned in a classroom. Being average is nothing to be ashamed of. We all have the same sort of bowl and over our lifetime it gets filled up. Or at least, all of the average people do.

There are outliers of course. Right up the top end of the bell curve. There is something different about their bowl. It is vast and voracious. Their bowl always seems to need more. In a very specific situation, if every hurdle is removed, if they have the time and the resources, their bowl will fill.

This traditionally will not happen very often. Humans are easily distracted with human pursuits like food and shelter and the chemistry with Erin in chemistry class. On the very rare occasion that it does happen, society lunges forwards. Big things get invented. Writing. The printing press. Physics that make sense. Physics that don't make sense. The Internet.

A single mutant human has an inspired moment and everyone else gets dragged along in their wake.

At Sea

Dave glanced back at the wake his sailboat cut through the impermanently passive Pacific. Salt water slapped against the custom built matte hull. The SatNav hummed to itself. Getting close. He drummed his fingers on the hull. The first thing anyone would notice about the boat was the colour. It was such a plain brown. No texture. No boards. He'd considered reprinting the whole boat with a wood grain embedded into the design but the tidiness of the effect had grown on him.

The boat silently adjusted its trim in reaction to the wind direction. He smiled and shifted his seat position back into the shade where his pale complexion could remain that way. That had been a fun project. A couple of sensors and servos and the whole boat could pilot itself. A 'bubblegum for the mind' activity. A nice distraction from the more complex problems that he'd committed himself to.

Like weather. The atmosphere was such a chaotic system. He'd become good at making predictions. Fashion trends, stock markets, global politics. The turbid rivers of energy and moisture in the air, however, had been quite the puzzle. He pressed his palms together and bounced his hands against his lips. His predictions were only slightly more accurate than those of the Australian Bureau of Meteorology. A terrible disappointment. None-the-less it was enough that he could chart a course across the Pacific that avoided all the storms and swells and only took him into rain to refresh his water stores.

The SatNav sang a gentle but insistent song. Of course there was no 'Sat' in his 'Nav'. He didn't like to be reliant on other people at the best of times and once he'd worked out how to account for the bob and swell his accelerometers did a fine job of keeping his position. This was the place. He pulled out his binoculars and scanned the horizon looking for the telltale splash of surf smashing against the rocky cays.

The lapping of the sea continued. Petrels described great arcs around the boat scanning the surface for startled flying fish. Flying fish beneath the waves stubbornly maintained a sense of composure and calm. Dave paused. There! He nudged the tiller into manual mode and bore down on his target making the remainder of his month long voyage in only minutes.

The rocky prominence punched its way out of the ocean like a fist. The volcanic processes that had squeezed this geology to the surface were competing with the weather and the waves keeping it only a metre above the high tide mark. It was perfect. He knelt down on the deck and knocked out a tattoo on the seamless surface. A click and a panel revealed. The tolerance was within microns. When it came to secret panels Dave did not mess around. What he was about to do was going to change everything and while the chance of some coast guard stumbling onto him had been remote there was no sense in taking unnecessary risks.

He swung the panel up, unclipped the glass cylinder inside and pulled it out into the sunlight. Silver grey liquid sloshed inside, twinkling in the harsh sun. He held it up to his eye and swilled it as if contemplating an expensive glass of Shiraz before hefting it back over his shoulder.

"This is for you Rabia"

The container dashed against the stones and spilled its contents into the cracks and crevices. The goo started to eat

into the hard stone. This fluid was hungry…
   …and very, very smart.

Rabia

"You need to be kinder to people"

Dave's heart hammered underneath his polo shirt. Rabia's palm was pressed on his chest.

"I am kind. But some people are…"

"Not as smart as you?"

"No one's as smart as me."

The afternoon sun drenched him with photons adding to the heat that was sizzling in his cheeks. Was it anger or embarrassment, he couldn't tell. Her dark eyes dared him to look directly at her. In a desperate attempt to step up to the challenge his line of sight darted around her face and head scarf. It was so hot he might combust. The sandstone facade of the Electrical Engineering building loomed over them both.

"You have great ideas" she said, "but no one will listen to you if you don't show them kindness."

"Why should I be kind to them when they're too stupid to understand?"

"Kindness isn't a reward for those who deserve it. It's a gift you give yourself."

He met her eyes for a split second as a new piece of information lodged in his mind. He could almost feel the sensation of a new network of dendrites coming alive in his brain. Something important had happened.

He wondered if his silence had become awkward for her and was unsurprised when she gave him two condescending pats on the chest, adjusted the backpack on her shoulder and turned to leave.

He watched her departure then stood a while thinking as the photons bounced off him and into the grass.

The following day she was folding herself into a classroom chair. It was one of those with an attachment that promised all of the benefits of a desk but fulfilled none of them whilst simultaneously taking the comforts of a chair and ruining those too. She caught the scent of jasmine when suddenly a bunch of lilacs were thrust under her nose.

"I just wanted to say 'Thank you' "

Rabia stared up in horror. This was not what she wanted. The other two girls in the class pressed their heads together and snickered at her misfortune.

"Why do these smell… like jasmine?"

"I thought the jasmine smelled better but the lilacs were prettier, so I spritzed them with jasmine perfume."

She narrowed her eyes.

"I want to thank you for what you said yesterday. It was really helpful and I decided to put it into effect."

"You really didn't have to buy me flowers. I just want you to stop being a jerk."

He shifted his gaze to the blooms in his hand.

"Oh! No, these aren't for you. Well, one of them is I guess."

He lifted up one from the posy and placed it in her fingers. Then, as suddenly as he'd arrived, he'd jostled away to give a flower each to the other girls. They looked at each other in shock and bemusement. The last stem was popped into the lecturer's dais before Dave himself pivoted into one of the 'seats of despair'. He plopped down his books and started making notes when a light lit up in his face.

"Hello, hello" he rounded on his seat mates.

Then just as suddenly back into his notes. He had whirled in like a fragrant tornado and suddenly it was calm again. The girl in front of her whispered something to her seat partner who giggled cruelly, but then, discretely, she took a satisfied sniff of her lilac and smiled.

'Damnit!' she thought to herself, 'I like him'.

And that would have been the most interesting part of her day but for them discovering the lecturer's fragrance allergy.

The Vending Machine

Footsteps skittered down the narrow alleyway. One of the most effective things human brains do is decode patterns. A primal part of Gustavo recognised the cadence of the foot falls, matched them with his friends and determined the intent. The instinctual systems of an eleven year old boy accelerated from bored to exuberant in a fraction of a second. Half-formed thoughts were left unfinished in his notebook and he was running with the rest of his pack. He couldn't hear what his grandfather called after him but he knew it would be 'Be home by dinner'.

Years of practice had the boys navigating the treacherous cobblestones like mountain goats. Grey haired tourists in crisp shirts crept along the paths. The influx of travellers drawn by the rich culture of Portugal had injected a small boost to the local economy. Hotels went up. Cafés took on extra staff and adjusted their menus to cater to the eager visitors. Tour busses filled the streets. The rich culture of course, never had a chance. It was jostled off the streets by hen's parties, café spruikers and happy hours.

"Where are we going?" Gustavo yelled.

"Someone found something in the river. My cousin said it was..."

The voice got lost in the hubbub. A pink cardboard thumbs-up on a pole indicated a tour-group being provided a mildly apocryphal tale about a local piece of architecture. Gustavo side-stepped and stumbled to avoid hitting the big white butts of the big white Brits. There on the ground lay a candy striped clutch purse. It must have been freshly dropped. Anything containing money didn't stay on the street for long. Especially in this part of town. He grabbed it and inside sat a fat handful of euros alongside a 'deck' of credit cards.

He snuck his hand in and grabbed the top card.

"Loren Holdsworth?" he read out loud.

"LOREN HOLDSWORTH??

A tanned woman in a big white hat turned around in shock. Her stocky partner also pivoted. Gustavo proffered the purse.

"You dropped this" he said in adorably accented English.

She snatched the purse and card back and her cheeks went red. A puffy gentleman with cheeks equally as red gently stepped to shield her. Gustavo opened his hands face up. He had read that this was the universal gesture of compliance used by all apes to suggest 'I have no weapon. Let us not kill each other'. Loren failed to discreetly check that the money was all still there.

"Did he take anything?" the man muttered.

"I don't think so" The puffy man leaned down and put a heavy hand on Gustavo's shoulder.

"Did you take anything mate?"

Gustavo leaned forward and met his gaze. His eyes beamed wide.

"It wasn't mine to take."

He'd seen this before. Tourists get anxious. They're wary of being cheated and he'd seen some pretty highly-strung miscommunications. When he'd stumbled onto the science of body language it felt like magic. The right tone. Eyes in a certain direction. All these tiny indications he'd learned to broadcast with his body. It was like making a puppet dance. A big angry puppet that could kill you.

"It's all here." Loren said. A heat of embarrassment tickled her cheeks.

Gustavo stepped back from the man's grip, and offered "Have a great holiday".

Loren plucked ten euros from her bundle to offer as thanks but when she looked up again he was gone.

Gustavo scrambled down into the shallows of the wide cool river and saw the box. He looked around for witnesses. Seagulls cried out for chips and an elderly boater just offshore was contentedly swearing and cutting the fishing line from his boat engine.

Whatever the box was, the older boys had got it upright in the shallows. It was shaped like a fridge.

"What's inside it?"

"It's stuck. I can't get it open."

One of the boats that ran tourists under the bridges of Porto passed by causing a wash to splash up against the box. It rocked forward threatening to crash face first before returning clownishly to its upright position.

"I think it's some sort of vending machine."

"Let me try. I want a coke."

The bright yellow four pointed star embossed on the front burst into light and a dozen children jumped backwards. The door was pulled open and light spilled out. Inside was a cold can of Coca-Cola. It was cracked open and shared around. None of them came from affluent backgrounds and flavoured drinks tended to be a rare treat but despite this no one claimed more than their fair share. It was soon empty. Gustavo noted a typo on the can.

'Coco-Colah'

"It's locked again"

"There wasn't anything else in there anyway"

"Get a stick or something."

Progressively muddier children took turns trying to break open the stubbornly affixed door.

"We need a crowbar."

Again the star lit up. A square with an arrow from each face. Gustavo thought it looked like directions on a map. North, west, east and south. The door swung open. There in the light, lay an iron crowbar. He grabbed the tool and, like a tiny Portuguese King Arthur lifted it over his head. Eleven pairs of eyes stared in bewilderment.

"We need to get this somewhere safe" he said.

"How are we supposed to get it up the bank?"

Gustavo turned towards the machine.

"We need," he said, terrified that this wouldn't work and the spell would be broken "a trolley for moving a drinks machine."

The star lit up for a third time.

Deported

Dave tapped in a code on his front door. The numbers were immaterial but the cadence of the tapping was measured and compared in a database entry and the door latch clicked. He stepped through his kitchen and the part of his brain that had evolved for hunting prey, once again filtered out such unimportant elements of his environment like the pile of dishes accruing on the sink.

Rabia was balled up on the couch.

"Sweetheart? What's wrong?"

"They're going to send me back. I know it! I can't go back."

Dave picked up the letter on the table. The Government of Australia stamp across the top of the page always gave his heart a little jump. He skimmed the page. Her temporary resident visa had not been renewed.

He hugged her tight. He wasn't much of a hugger but he was getting better at reading the situation. Humans were just like computers. Put the right input in and you tended to get the right output. Of course, there was a lot of bug fixing first.

"I'm sure we can get this reviewed. You are so bright. This country would be lucky to have you."

"They hate me!"

"They don't hate you."

"They hate all brown people!"

"They don't... *all* hate you. They fear you."

"But why? I'm not scary."

"Australia is a safe place. We've never had real things to be frightened of."

"Their biggest fear" she spat with tears in her eyes, "is that they'll find out they don't deserve what they have."

Dave snatched up the form and scoured it for a contact number.

"I'm going to get this sorted out. This is just like any other problem. I just have to work out the inputs and outputs."

He picked up the phone and entered the Department of Immigration phone number for the first time.

"We are currently experiencing unusually high call volumes. We thank you for your patience."

Dave searched for the definition of the word 'unusually' on his computer to double check its meaning. His brain felt like a pit-bull whose chain has wrapped around his doghouse during a thunderstorm. Scared, angry and impotent.

Two days he'd been playing their game. Phone messages, transfers, dropped calls and this. Call waiting. Every two minutes the music would repeat. Like a Chinese water torture dripping into his ears. Then the incessant reminders, each time promising a human response. 'Click'…

"Hello? I…"

"Welcome to the Department of Immigration. We are currently experiencing…"

He pondered what sort of team was involved in the creation of such a torturous system. Had it been meticulously planned out to create as much frustration as possible? Was the design to prefer deportation and a possible death sentence rather that sit through another 95 seconds of digital saxophone? The job market was hard. There were desperate people everyone. Could anyone be desperate enough to take the job of 'State sponsored irritant'?

He pushed the heels of his hands against his eyeballs as if trying to push the tiredness back into his brain. The horror of losing the love of his life to bureaucracy had cut into his usual sleep schedule. It wasn't a great excuse, but it's the only one he really had for what he did next.

```
SELECT * in users WHERE name = 'rabia bishara';
name: rabia bishara dob: 1998-05-02 visa:
temporary temp_renewal_exp: 0 status: denied
UPDATE users SET status = 'current',
temp_renewal_exp = 800 WHERE name = 'rabia
bishara';
```

It had taken him all of eight minutes to hack into the government database and most of that was spent trying to remember the SQL update syntax. No more aural torture. A simple fix. In and out like a thief in the night.

"All fixed."

"What? How? Really?"

"I just got through to the right… person." he said.

"Oh my god! Dave, you're amazing. I'm so relieved."

Rabia burst into tears. He hugged her.

"Another 800 days on your visa. Hopefully we won't have such a covertly racist government by then."

She hugged into him with all her strength. They celebrated with dinner out. When they returned home Dave fell asleep when his head hit the pillow.

He awoke in the predawn and pondered his reckless solution. He really hadn't been at his best. Perhaps he should jump back in now that his brain was a little more focused and make sure he'd covered his tracks. It took him longer this time. It was important to be thorough. This was, after all, technically a federal crime. First to make sure there were no backup systems doing parity checks and overwriting his change.

```
SELECT 'status' in users WHERE name = 'rabia
bishara';
status: high_alert
```

Oh… no.

Federal police at the front door entered the code 1111. The rhythmic pattern of 'THUD THUD THUD THUD(snap)' was enough to bypass the database and, it turned out, the door frame. There were many times in his life that Dave had yearned to be in just his underpants. As six armed policeman burst into his house at 5am he concluded that this was not one of them.

There was a scream from the bedroom as the number of machine guns present rose above zero. Dave lay down in the carpet and put his hands on his head. A deep shame bloomed inside him. With his face pressed into the synthetic threads he noticed, possibly for the first time in his life, that perhaps he should do the vacuuming.

Nintondo

"I did not raise my child to be a thief!"

Diogo, tried to make himself as small as possible as his father's wrath and spittle rained down upon him.

"Look at me when I'm talking to you! What do you think your grandmother would say if she saw you right now? She would die all over again of shame."

Diogo's grandmother 'Vo-vo' sold bootleg cherry liqueur on her front stoop for the best part of her final decade. Diogo felt that she had a moral compass but that it would spin wildly whenever she travelled through her own personal Bermuda triangle.

He decided to keep this information to himself. The phrase 'This logical argument has reduced my anger' was one that he'd never heard his father utter.

"I didn't steal it. It was... a gift"

The world turned a whitish-black for a split second as this father's open hand slapped his face.

"A thief AND a liar?! Tell me the truth or I shall send you to meet your grandmother."

"It's a machine. We found it at the river. It gives you whatever you ask it for. The other boys told me to keep it a secret."

"A machine that dispenses Nintendos for free? Your mouth is a drain of lies."

"Look! It's not a Nintendo."

He turned it over and there on the label it stated

'Nintondo'.

"We compared it to the ones in the shop. The only difference is the name, the copyright notice and the 'Made in Japan' line."

"Where is this machine?"

"I can't tell you. Gu..."

He zipped his mouth shut. He was already in trouble with one person. Best to keep it that way. His father's cheeks flushed and he grabbed Diogo's ear and forced him down the stairs of their apartment.

"You'll do as I tell you boy! Now lead the way."

They navigated the weaving streets down to an abandoned boathouse nestled between two other abandoned boathouses. All rotten boards splattered with seagull droppings. The chatter of the tourists on the main streets had evaporated leaving only the creaking of wood and rope and water.

Diogo gave a shameful sniff as his father pushed his shoulder up against the heavy door and shoved it aside. Inside lay a boy's wonderland. Rows of TVs and gaming devices, a pinball machine, a stereo, coloured lamps and a surprising amount of state of the art cleaning equipment. Up against the wall was a vending machine with a four pointed star.

"How does it work?"

Diogo stood in front of it sniffling and stuttered out "Please give me a Nintendo Switch."

He didn't need to say 'please', but his Vo-vo had taught him that 'being polite when you don't need to never got anyone into trouble'.

The front of the machine bloomed white. A click. Diogo handed his father what claimed to be a 'Nendindo' console. The box was strong and light. At closer inspection it wasn't cardboard. More like a thin fibreglass. The words 'Please recycle' glimmered across the vending machine in the local language before vanishing again.

Diogo had never seen his father happy to receive something from him before.

"Ask for something you'd like" said Diogo.

His father stood quietly for moment and then hesitantly uttered "I want a Beretta 92".

The machine hummed, glowed and clicked. The door opened and he picked up the high powered pistol. It was warm to the touch.

"Jesus" he whispered under his breath.

He yanked out his phone, "Valdemar! I need you to come help me move something"

"Dad! No please!"

Diogo's father put his hand over the mouthpiece and squatted down to be face to face with his son.

"Listen to me. Don't tell anyone about this. Not your friends, not your mother, no one. If you keep the secret you can keep the console. If you don't, I shall beat you within an inch of your life. Understand."

Diogo nodded.

Before long Valdemar arrived. The machine was loaded up and taken away in a van.

When the room was silent again Gustavo crept out of the shadows. They'd made a pact. Keep everything silent. Never take anything from this room. Don't tell anyone. Thanks to Diogo they hadn't made it a week. Gustavo trudged home, past his sleeping grandpa and into his bedroom. He opened up his cupboard. Inside was a vending machine with a yellow pointed star on the front. The machine that had washed up in the river had a cavity around a metre and a half in height. This was ever so slightly shorter than that. It looked like offspring, and in a way, it was.

The front panel pulsed. Please recycle. Require: gold, silicon, lithium, boron…

Chat

Dave went to drum out his password on the entry pad before realising the front door was ajar and partly off its hinges. 'To serve and protect' did not extend to craftsmanship it seemed. The living room was covered in loose paper. What sort of job was it to have to rummage professionally? Meticulously scouring piles of paperwork for suspicious content and then casting it aside in a manner not at all meticulous.

Whether or not they found anything worth taking, Dave couldn't tell. His filing method involved giving anything important to the computer and outsourcing the crucial job of forgetting about it to the silicon. Dusty patterns on the cheap chipboard desk outlined the absence of his computer and backup drives. His online backup provider promised he wouldn't lose anything of value. He supposed that didn't include the loss of the love of his life.

He allowed himself a little cry.

He forced his breathing to slow, tucked the emotions down and turned his mind to solving the problem. The first thing he needed to do was get online. The bottom drawer of his desk was hanging open. A nest of cables wove together in a knot of some resolve. Like an archeologist chipping back through historical epochs Dave finally found a Palm Treo circa 2007. He sat on the couch in the fading afternoon light and pecked away with a small plastic stylus.

He'd thrown together a simple secure chat program of his own design. He wasn't about to trust his private nothings to

the corporations and so he had 'rolled his own'. He and Rabia
had often wasted away the evenings of their courtship
volleying jokes and insights back and forth across the virtual
net. More recently it was clustered with shopping lists and
dinner decisions.

'I will find you.' he tapped out on the grainy screen.

He didn't know how, but it was the greatest drive inside
himself he'd ever felt and he was going to dedicate himself to
it. He stared at the screen. Quietly the room went dark as he
waited for the pulsing three dots. He didn't know whether
they would return her phone to her or where she was even
being held. Australia's government wasn't all phone trees
and red tape. Buoyed up by the "success" of Brexit a few
years prior, Prime Minister Dutton had fast-tracked his
border-security bill through and the whole thing had become
a nightmare for anyone that didn't look like him. ie. a waxed
vizier.

She could be on Christmas island by morning. He grabbed
a can of chickpeas from the cupboard to fuel himself and set
to work making notes. It was just a problem. And all
problems had a solution.

He awoke in the predawn momentarily confused as to
where his bed was and why it had been replaced with a
couch covered in chickpea brine. He jabbed at the old PDA
and it's backlight popped on.

'They're sending me back to Iran'

'I'm at the airport. I stole a phone'

'I don't blame you'

'I lobbe yuu'

'qw345y66666'

The messages stopped. Dave's breath fell into the depths of

his stomach. Iran. Rabia had told him what would happen if she ever set foot on that soil again. What could he do? He bought a plane ticket.

The Scrap Boy

Gustavo climbed the cobblestones dragging his trolley behind. He'd decided on a smooth green cart with big bicycle wheels. The two long handles protruding forwards gave by-passers the impression of a 'Gustavo drawn' carriage. Tidy white letters on the side proclaimed 'Porto scrap and recycling project'. He caught the eye of a painter. The old tradesman pinched off his cigarette and dropped it in an old jam jar.

"Got yourself a man's job there" he chuckled.

"Do you have any empty paint pots you need to get rid of, sir?"

"Ya can't dump this stuff. I'm supposed to take these to some plant out in the outskirts of town to make sure it's disposed of correctly. Hell of a job."

"I can take it sir. This new recycling program can deal with old paint."

"No shit? Yeah great. Uh, those ones over there. Anything with its cap off."

Gustavo piled the empty cans into the tray of his cart. If they were hard to recycle then that meant there was probably something the box was craving. He pulled out a wrapped basket. The wrapping paper was bright and clean. It felt strange to touch, like it was slightly elastic. It was only by very careful examination that you'd see the tiny lattice work, like origami hexagons etched in the fibres. He passed it to the painter.

"What's this?"

"Part of the program sir. A gift box. Soap. Toilet paper. Razors."

"I don't have any money sorry"

"It's free. It's a thank you from the program."

"For a bunch of old cans?"

"It's yours. No strings attached."

He took the basket like it was about to wake up and attack him then carefully peeled open the wrapping to peer in. He would later discover that this simple unbranded razor would last longer that it had any right to. He looked down at Gustavo then dug into his overalls and pulled out a card so wrinkled that it may well have been called 'casual' rather than 'business'.

"There's heaps where that came from son. Pop around on Thursday and load up."

Gustavo thanked the man, plunged the card into his pocket and returned to his trip up the hill. Quiet electric motors kicked in and he barely needed to touch the handles for the whole device to follow at his heels like a puppy. He felt strongly about the gift basket. He knew that he was helping people but all the same, they had no idea how valuable their detritus was. The gift basket felt like a payment. He'd considered offering money. The machine would provide that just as easily as anything else. He'd mulled over the pros and cons and it quickly occurred to him that he'd never heard of a soap and toilet-paper counterfeiter going to jail. Yes, best to provide high quality household products for now.

The architecture became more ornate as he climbed. It defied Newtonian physics but wealth, it seemed, flowed uphill. He stopped at an ornate white door. Beautiful Madeira Bell-heathers bloomed in pots under the street facing window. He pressed on the doorbell and an expensive chime rang out. A moment later and a middle aged woman cautiously peered through a crack in the door. Gustavo gave his warmest smile.

"Good morning Ma'am. Porto scrap and recycling project. Do you have any waste products you need removed?"

Firearms

Erico wondered if Valdemar's heart was thumping like his was. He'd dealt with some shady people before but these guys were positively overcast. He looked awkwardly down at his clothing and, for the first time, wandered if it was too ostentatious. The machine had given them everything they'd asked for up to and including Chinchilla fur coats and gold chains.

In a rather short sighted manner they'd also asked for thousands of euros. The wads of bills appeared when they opened the door but their excitement was short lasted. €123 notes. Purple notes. His stomach lurched when he found a note where the usual architecture had been replaced with an image of his home address.

No matter. Gold had value anywhere. Pure gold did at any rate. The jeweller took one look at the small gold ingot they'd provided and immediately felt the lack of heft. A quick check and it became obvious this was gold plated. A microscopically thin costume of gold around any old worthless alloy. One small bribe later and the police were not called for what the jeweller presumed was an intentional ruse.

They rushed back to the flat and this time asked for 'pure' gold. The door opened there in the centre was a small gold button. It almost disappeared between his thumb and forefinger. This machine his son's friends had discovered was like some sort of cruel genie. Erico slammed the door again but before he could ask for more gold the display lit up.

Please recycle. Require: gold… gold… gold..

Erico's neighbours heard a short burst of profanity.

But the guns had value. He and Valdemar had the machine create a small arsenal the first day they'd taken the machine. They'd spent the afternoon at the old quarry with a six pack of beer and a backpack full of pistols and ammo the machine had happily expelled for them. No old can was safe.

Valdemar had set up a meeting with some friends of friends. Erico muttered out the side of his mouth to his partner in crime.

"Friends of friends?"

"Well, maybe acquaintances of acquaintances"

Aloisio Barbozo had his man open the crate. He was the sort of criminal who had a man and also, it seemed, the sort of criminal who met in creepy old warehouses infested with pigeons. Erico and Valdemar had asked the machine for a crate of guns. It had provided 2 dozen pistols of various design, a collapsed rack and a folded up charcoal grey box. They'd unfolded it and slid the rack into the box. The design was stylish. Like an apple product. Aloisio was impressed.

"Stolen?"

Erico tried to find his voice.

"N.. No"

The stoic gangster stayed very still and left a thick silence to fill.

"We… d.. didn't steal them. They were… made for us."

Aloisio picked out a pistol and slid a magazine into it.

"I would like to know", he said as the magazine clicked in "Who made them for you?"

Erico glaced at Valdemar who imperceptibly shook his head.

"That's not important!" he tried.

He wished his heartbeat would soften. It felt harder and

harder to hear anything else.

"I would like to know" Aloisio firmly stated as he decreased the distance between them, "Who is making guns and off loading them in my city? I know about all the gun running in Porto and you two amateurs waltz in and try to upend the game? Who MADE THEM FOR YOU!!"

Erico looked into the barrel of the pistol. He desperately tried to inhale his tears back into his eyeballs.

"The machine!" Valdemar yelled surprising even himself.

"Please don't kill us. There's a machine that will give you anything you ask of it. We asked it for guns. We just wanted to sell you some guns to make some money."

Aloisio frowned. "Why would you need money if you have a machine that makes you anything?"

There was a pause while metaphorical dots got joined.

"In any event" said Aloisio, "I control the supply of weapons in this city, and you're being taken out of the equation."

His raised the pistol and pulled the trigger.

There was a pop. Erico didn't have a chance to realise he'd been shot before realising that he hadn't. Everyone looked at the flag that had erupted from the pistol. In large brash lettering it read 'Blam!'

The scene was so absurd. Like a frozen moment in a comic book. Somewhere a pigeon cooed. Valdemar took off at speed. Erico was the next to recover his senses and away he sprinted. He heard the ricochet of bullets as they darted into the laneways. Growing up here at least gave them the advantage of knowing the shortcuts. His lungs pumped poison and he felt like his heart would finally give up when they burst into the crowds of tourists. They waited until they were sure there were no pursuers.

"We tested every single gun" said Valdemar.

"That fucking machine" responded Erico, "is a curse. I'm

going to break the damn thing down into parts."

He was sore, and tired and had the distinct impression he needed a change of underwear. These distractions were such that he didn't notice the police cars until he was almost inside his building. The door opened and a startled officer confronted him.

"Erico Pereyra? We'd like to ask some questions pertaining to some counterfeit currency reported to us by a local jeweller."

"What… uh, makes you think I had anything to do with it?"

The officer held up the €200 note. There, instead of the watermarked face of the Phoenician princess Europa there was a clear and entirely incriminating picture of Erico Pereyra. Erico slowly turned on Valdemar.

"Well, I wasn't going to bribe him with real money." said Valdemar.

The policeman made a note in his notepad.

"Uhh, you don't need to write that down."

The policeman made a note in his notepad.

Leaking Borders

"Heading 335"

Captain Ian Thompson lifted his binoculars to his face and tracked the horizon for his prey. Recruits in Operation Sovereign Borders often didn't last long. Weeks at sea at a time. Long stretches of boredom and short bursts of action. There was an emotional weight to being tasked to destroy what little hope the weak and persecuted had. It cut short many promising careers. Captain Thompson had seen a great deal of turnover while he climbed the ranks. He liked to think that there was a special fire inside him that made him particularly suited to the job. His stoicism. His level head. Also, it helped that he was very racist. The look of pleading on the tear stained cheeks of young women who had lost everything only served to buoy his spirits. He was everything the current Australian Government could hope for.

The Liberal National Party had, many years ago promised to 'Turn Back the Boats'. He couldn't believe the brazenness of it. It was one step back from 'Turn Back the Blacks' and yet the population had run with it. He'd fallen so deeply into despair that the PC culture was infringing on his freedoms and yet here was proof that he wasn't alone. He put in his request for transfer the next day.

Over the years he'd risen through the ranks. The operation had been successful. Too successful. Indonesian people smugglers had all but given up and most of his job was cruising endless seas. But today was special. Radars had picked up a bogie. There, amongst the seabirds, blinking in and out behind the swell, was a boat full of bludgers. Ocean scum. Queue jumpers. This was going to be a joy.

"Get the ducks ready" he called over his shoulder.

"Yes Captain Tommo".

When he'd taken the command he'd wanted to bond with his crew. To instil a sense of Aussie pride. He'd insisted they call him Tommo. It had lasted all of 45 minutes before an official missive had gone out requiring the 'Captain' prefix be returned.

His crew moved like clockwork. Two teams would load into a pair of Futuro Commando rigid body inflatable boats. They'd pull alongside the scared and hungry passengers and dash their plans to sponge off the hard working quiet Australians. His heart filled with pride displacing what others suggested was coal. As they got close it seemed like something was wrong with the boat. Was it sinking? The swell undulated and he saw it. A second boat? Jackpot! What a feather in his cap. Two boats travelling so close they were practically on top of each other. They slid behind the swell again.

Perhaps Prime Minister Dutton would even mention him by name. Captain Tommo. The thin grey line between black and white. He adjusted his binoculars. Where... had those vessels gone?

"Radar?"

"They've gone dark sir"

He stared at the frustratingly unoccupied patch of ocean as it resolutely remained empty.

"Bloody oath" he muttered patriotically.

Welcome Aboard

Sunny sat in the darkness. Her mind raced to the stories of sea monsters her grandfather had told when she was a toddler. Something had swallowed them.

The trip had been calmer than she expected. She'd been warned by her parents that the seas could be frightening but the whole experience had been tedious if anything. And then the seas had picked up. Rolling hills of water and power. Some passengers turned quite pale but Sunny had loved it. Down into the gutter and then just as fast up the other side.

"A boat!" she'd called in delight.

Very quickly the mood changed. Other passengers started shouting. The pilot was quick to disarm the anxiety.

"They probably won't see us in these seas. Look, they're sailing past."

Everyone's eyes watched as the massive naval vessel's silhouette changed from wide and pointy, to just plain pointy. She'd seen the terrifying advisements on televisions at home. The Australian Government promised to catch them and tow them back. Sunny's mother started to cry. On the horizon the Australian ship remained distant but closing. There was sudden yelling and the skies went black. The yelling continued for a moment then died away.

Someone held their mobile phone up to illuminate the cabin. All eyes darted around trying to make sense of their surroundings. The swell had stopped. The lapping of water died away replaced with a low hum. Sunny peered out the window trying to make out the shape of the monsters belly. She was dazzled when the darkness fractured and elegant neon blue handwriting appeared. It spiralled across the void and etched the words 'You are Safe' first in English, then in Indonesian and a handful of other languages she didn't recognise.

It continued, 'Please be calm and quiet'.

They waited. In the minutes that followed anxious whispering began. One of the older passengers began to make herself heard. It was always the elderly whose patience for rules and advisements ran out first. That sense that 'they knew better'. Just because they'd 'been around a long time' Sunny pondered to herself 'didn't mean they'd spent all that time making good decisions'. The writing mostly faded leaving only the word 'quiet'. It then added two underlines. There was shushing and even the grey noise was quelled.

The hum intensified. Whatever they were in, it was accelerating. Fifteen minutes later the whole room lit up. It looked like a space ship. Their rickety fishing vessel had been hugged by a collection of inflatable pads. The water they'd sailed in on had drained away leaving only a matte charcoal floor. A catwalk reached around the boat and in the walls of the vessel were bunk beds. Towards the front was seating and what looked like a vending machine with a shining yellow compass rose on it.

The flat walls above the bunk beds curved into the ceiling. Shapes folded and unfolded across the whole surface until the whole room was covered in coloured rectangles. Each shape flickered and became a screen with the same face on it. The background hum softened and stopped and the screens started to play.

"Good afternoon travellers to Australia. You have been intercepted by a New Pangaea advocate vessel. You have been promised a better life in Australia. We regret to inform you that the life promised to you there is all but impossible. Previous travellers have ended their journey in offshore detention centres and the current success rate of finding a comfortable home is less than one percent. Your boat was moments away from being intercepted and removed from Australian waters."

Video clips replaced the face. Filthy accommodation. Hopeless refugees. Military might.

"New Pangaea would like to offer you an alternative. If you have plans to return to your country of departure or you are set on continuing to Australia your captain will be returned to the sea and you may accompany them. New Pangaea offers the lifestyle that you were promised. You do not need to make the decision right now though. Please come aboard and enjoy our hospitality. Request the meal of your choice from our 'Combobulator'. Take this moment to relax and get yourself a good night's sleep. There's a big decision to make tomorrow."

The face faded and the shapes disappeared into the ceiling. For a moment no-one moved. Then a surprisingly spry grey blur rushed passed. The chatty elderly woman scrambled out of the boat, onto the catwalk and collapsed into a chair. Sunny couldn't understand the language that was spoken but the intent was obvious. This was the first day all week she had proper lumbar support and it was bliss.

The 'Combobulator' turned out to be easy to use and within moments a line had formed as the voyagers selected the meal that they most craved. Sunny stood quietly watching the magic happen. A cheer would go up whenever the door opened and the challenge set to it had been met. The boat quickly filled with the smells of curries and fried chicken. Sunny asked politely for her meal and sat next to her parents.

"Sunny! Pie? You can't have just dessert for dinner." her mother chided.

"It's a special occasion dear. Let her indulge herself this once."

"Mother, it's not a dessert."

She'd been looking forward to this moment since her parents first talked to her about this undertaking. She knew exactly what she wanted the machine to serve her. Thick red sauce oozed from the small glass saucière and covered her very first Australian meat pie. If New Pangaea could get this right she didn't care where it was.

Evidence

Detective Machado quietly locked the door from the inside. He moved close to his superior. They stood silently in the evidence lock-up staring at the Portuguese tarts that sat in the bottom of the machine. Principal Detective Carrico slowly leaned down and picked one up.

"What are you doing?" whispered Machado?

Carrico bit into the tart and let out an appreciative hum.

"Izzo good!" he happily muttered as crumbs threw themselves desperately from his lips.

Machado picked up the second tart and took a cautious sniff. It smelled really good. Not this dross that they foisted on the tourists. This was a proper tart. He took a bite.

"Oh my goodness!"

"I know, right!"

"How does it do that? How does it heat them so quickly? Is it baking them? Where did it come from? What else can it make?"

"That's probably the most important question."

Carrico closed the door and addressed the machine.

"I would like 100 grams of cocaine and a Smith & Wesson Bodyguard 38."

The machine glowed for a moment. The door clicked. Carrico open the machine and swore. The revolver felt heavy in his hand. He flipped it open. It was empty. Machado picked up what looked like a packet of cigarettes and read the label.

"Cocaine! It says in a fancy font. Two 25mg serves. Class 2 controlled substance. Danger! Please check local laws in relation to narcotics. Do not take more often than once per week. Not to be taken with other narcotics. Not to be taken with alcohol. Cocaine use can damage your sinuses. Cocaine can be a dangerous substance if taken in large quantities. Cocaine is very addictive. We recommend instead selecting Psilocybin or MDMA for your recreational drug needs."

Carrico balked "You've got to be shitting me!"

"Please recycle this packaging"

"It doesn't say that."

"It does! Right there"

Carrico let back his head and let out a dark bawdy laugh.

"I wonder", he mused "if it's as good as the tart."

They opened the pack. Inside he found two transparent vials of white powder. Warnings covered the packaging. Carrico barked at the machine to give him another. It glowed for a moment and behind the door he found a small card the read 'Recommended dose. No more than two lines per week'.

"So it's a drug machine with a conscience."

"What the hell do we do with it? This thing is invaluable."

"I'll work out a way to lock it closed. You take that," he nodded at the vial in Machado's hand "down to forensics. Now how the hell am I going to do this?"

He started looking around the room for a chain and lock.

Machado addressed the machine "Give me a lockable harness that fits this device."

The machine glowed. Machado grinned and gave a big thumbs up as he dashed out of the room.

Detective Machado stepped into the forensics lab for the second time that day. It always made him feel proud. Testimony was fine, but scientific evidence lodged in a jury's mind like crystal. It wasn't the most well-financed lab in town but they did good work.

"Same day service KC?" he said. "To what do I owe the honour?"

KC skittered into the front room.

"Machado!" she yipped "Where on Earth did you get this?"

"Need to know KC. What have you got for me?"

She roundly rounded her round face upon him.

"This cocaine…"

"Good?"

"100% pure. You take double what you've given me and you could be in real trouble. Users aren't used to the pure stuff. If they enjoy 4 lines of this their heart's gonna pop."

"I thought that might be the case." he said reflecting on the tart.

"But that's not the weirdest thing. I transferred the contents of the vial to test it and as I emptied it I tapped it."

She tapped the glass vial on the table for effect.

'bink bink'

"I've tapped a lot of glass containers and nothing rings like that. So I took a closer look at the glass under a microscope."

"It's not glass?"

"It's diamond."

"WHAT?!"

"Lab grown diamond. No flaws. It gets weirder."

"How?"

"The box it came in. It's not cardboard. It's graphene."

"Graphene?"

"You must of heard of this stuff. It's a super strong substance made by organising carbon into a special lattice. You know diamonds are made by compressing carbon at high pressure? Graphene is like that but with a different molecular layout. It's one of those super materials that always seems to be 10 years away from consumer products. This stuff is graphene fibre woven into a stiff card."

"Expensive?"

"I'm holding hundreds of thousands of euros worth of product here. The pure coke is the cheapest part of the whole package."

Machado stroked his stubble.

"Maybe we should have a closer look at those counterfeit bank notes."

The List

Gustavo sat at his window and watched the sunrise. Oranges and pinks crammed their way into the early morning shadows like a Mardi Gras terminating at a goth club. It had been an upsetting morning. He'd awoken to the sound of retching and coughing. His grandfather had been enjoying these past few months of unrestricted access to his favourite foods. Gustavo's story was that his recycling job was providing enough pay to keep them neck deep in chorizo and wine.

The reality was that his mini-sized machine seemed to be able to create most food stuff with a minimum of elements. He'd worked out that their favourite meals were mostly carbon and he suspected that this was being filtered out of the air. The cloying miasma in the flat seemed somehow lighter. The quiet vent on top of the machine seemed to bleed fresh air into the room and he supposed the carbon dioxide and pollutants were all being sequestered for other purposes.

The thing that had caught him off-guard, was exactly what recycled elements allowed access to which foods. The machine wouldn't even provide water for him until it had enough calcium, magnesium and potassium. He would ask for something basic. Almonds. Where the machine's simple flat grey surface existed a moment before there lit up an ingredient list. Calcium, Copper, Iron, Phosphorus…

He'd loaded the machine with various rocks and scrap from the river bank and many of the warnings had silenced.

Then he would ask for something new, in one case salmon, and the machine would baulk and require selenium. Gustavo's knowledge of chemistry was racing ahead.

He requested a checklist of missing elements from the machine and it had provided a smooth sheet of the curiously strong cardboard it preferred. The full periodic table was etched in the surface, a large X crossing out the items he had already entered. This final row had many instances of 'NA'. These were elements the machine didn't need, he guessed. His next goal, silicon, was easy to source. He fed it into the machine before realising it was one of the elements already marked off his list.

He had been worried about gold but it turned out that old computer components were very easy to recover. Recycling them by traditional means involved a lot of heat and waste. His little vending machine did it quietly and calmly. He checked the list and gold had also already been checked off. He boggled. He knew he hadn't done gold yet. And there was palladium and tantalum also crossed off. He tossed in a hard drive and watched the card. Before his eyes an X embossed itself across 'neodymium'.

It could communicate wirelessly to its creations? Wow! Not for the first time Gustavo caught himself wishing for some sort of user's manual. This rectangular genie was a mess of secrets. He 'donked' himself on the forehead and turned to address the machine.

"I would like a user's manual for...", he stumbled "yourself?"

The machine glowed and the familiar yellow compass shape pulsed.

It became a game. A scavenger hunt. He'd considered

getting other boys in on the project but Diogo's treachery had him thinking twice. The weeks progressed and the machine was complaining less and less. There were however, some elements that eluded him. He doubted he'd need much radioactive matter but there were a handful that he'd never even heard of. What the heck was 'Thulium'?

The summer afternoons had been fresh and filled with light. His grandfather had told him stories from the war and they'd supped on their favourite foods. As the nights got longer his grandfather's health began to slip. Gustavo was able to provide the medication he needed but every clock eventually winds down.

One evening he'd opened his closet to ask the machine for cough syrup and it was already glowing. He opened it and inside was a card. It said, 'You have been cordially invited to… handout.miracle.algorithm'. That was it. No address. No details. Just a sparse invitation. There was a retching from the other room. He tucked the card into the user manual and resolved to ponder it later.

The coughing got worse but it was the gasping that chilled him to his core. That wheeze of someone ravenous for breathe. The final night Gustavo mopped his brow and held his hand. That was all he could do. There was pain, and fear and eventually an empty calm.

The town was starting to wake up and Gustavo distantly watched the early birds of Porto take to the streets. People calling out greetings and laughing. It was like they didn't even realise that his family, all the people in this world that loved him… they were all gone.

The Cage

Jason Mueller walked into the lab and tossed his tie onto the back of a chair. He popped his top button open and read the brief again. 'Nano-fabrication technology discovered in Portugal, Chad and Uruguay. CIA requires full tear-down and report on the potential for disruption'.

He rounded on the large Faraday cage. The fabrication device in question was illuminated on all sides by halogen lamps giving the impression of a trendy product shoot. Six and a half feet tall. 240 pounds. Grey glossy features with an embossed yellow… It looked like a compass rose. It was a yellow square with a small yellow arrow erupting from each side. A reverse image search had established it not as a logo at all but as a mock-up for a nanotech warning label.

He stepped into the cage. The agency's first attempt to extradite the box had failed at the border. A team had managed to grab one of them from Uruguay. They'd been forbidden from using the machine for their own personal whims and so it was with some comical confusion that the agents involved had been able to alert their superiors that the machine had stopped working moments after trucking it across the border into Argentina. It had taken a Faraday cage to cut the machine off from whatever tether it had to the outside world.

Disruptive technology had a way of shuffling the power of countries. Rome had paved roads. Europe had the printing press. Someone had decided to give this brand new power to a handful of very small players in the game. The United States were still top of the deck but this unassuming grey box could change all that. He ran a hand-held light along the edges of the device. No screws. No seams. The 'Right to Repair' people would be horrified. He knelt down to check underneath and spotted something rather odd. A black tendril running along the floor. He checked the photos on his laptop. That definitely hadn't been there before. He traced it to the tip and watched carefully. The clock in his classrooms at school had no second hand. In those last few minutes of the day he'd watch the tip of the big hand crawl excruciatingly towards the twelve. He was reminded of that moment as this wire grew across the tiles. An antenna! This damned machine was trying to phone home. He unhooked a set of pliers from his belt and clipped the line at the base.

The afternoon progressed. Jason ran a small rotary saw along the rear side edge then along the top. It was slow going. This looked and felt like perspex but it was something else entirely. Once he got to the bottom of the second edge he attempted to pry back the panel only to discover that the first edge had healed shut. The gaping wound he'd inflicted was stitching itself back together in front of his astonished face.

"Right! Going to be like that, are we?"

He requisitioned some pneumatic jaws and pulled out his collapsible cot. Someone had put a lot of trouble into making sure this cornucopia was location locked and he wanted to know why. The incisions he'd made were almost entirely healed. He ran his fingers along the almost invisible seam that remained and spotted two new antennae making a break for it along the floor. Two snips and they were taken care of. He stepped back and saw a message written on the machine. 'Danger: Signal failure. Machine must have signal to remain in safe mode.'

"Nice try mystery box" he said to the upset machine.

By dinner time he'd worked out the schedule. He pushed the branded takeaway bag to the corner of his desk and double checked his notes. The wires were growing at around twelve inches every hour. If he set an alarm every four hours he should be able to get some decent sleep and still have a couple of hours wiggle room to clip them short. The lights in the room were dimmed and he made himself comfortable on the thin camping mattress. From this angle he could still see into the cage and under the machine.

"Idiot!" he whispered to himself.

He clambered to his feet and unlocked the cage before pressing his nose to the floor again. Was the device smart enough to tunnel through the floor? Ten minutes later it was hanging from a hoist and deposited gently onto two concrete blocks. The cot was dragged into the cage and he took up position next to the machine. He reassured himself that the seconds on his timer were ticking down and then dropped his head onto the pillow where he fell into a deep sleep filled with visions of jungle and anacondas.

The alarm roused him and he grabbed at his phone. 10:18? He'd barely been asleep an hour. It took a moment before he realised the alarm wasn't coming from his phone, but from the machine itself. The plain grey surface was now pulsing in an urgent pillar-box red. The whole box seemed somehow more formidable. The base was thicker with great boils erupting from it. Jason tried to struggle to his feet. His legs didn't seem to want to wake up. He pushed himself up with all three hands. Three? He was dreaming. The machine had oozed across the floor and had consumed his legs. He flailed. As unreal as this was, it wasn't unreal enough to not be actually happening right now. A surge of half-dissolved takeaway threatened escape as he digested the horror of his predicament. He needed help. 'No Service' pulsed mockingly from his phone. Error messages cascaded down the front of the machine. 'Heartbeat s^^gnal not det8cted. DangER!'. It was harder and harder to catch his breath. He ripped at his shirt and found more fingers clutching and wriggling on his torso. One of them wore the same scar he had on his right hand. On both of his right hands.

"help!" he whispered as his lungs turned into a bubbling paste.

With horrible clarity he realised what was happening. The nanotech had mutated. It would eat and eat and eat turning everything into itself. Nothing could stop it. The world would soon become an undulated mass of nanotechnology battling to consume itself.

Grey goo.

His vision turned red and then black.

The alarms warbled to themselves and Jason Mueller's body grew more and more fingers and arms. The machine had any number of thin black cables spanning to the sky from its scintillating surface. At long last an antenna got free of the Faraday cage. In a snap the alarm stopped.

Silence.

Slowly, very slowly, the panels of the box reverted to their original form. Organic blisters sluiced off and onto the floor where they quietly transformed into sparkling dust. When Jason was found the following morning his body was already sealed up inside an airtight bag.

Autopsy results: Jason Mueller.
External Appearance:
-       34 year old white male with abnormal growths in

armpit and chest.

- Previously undiagnosed polymelia resulting in 7 arms and 67 extra fingers.
- Apparent prior amputation of legs with sponge-like residual limb.
- Lungs and diaphragm sponge-like with multiple perforations and tearing.

Probable cause of death: Asphyxiation

Extra notes:

- The entire surface of skin is tattooed in a repeating pattern.
- Tattoo is 3/4 inch across.
- Vibrant yellow outline of a square with an arrow pointing from each side.

Handout Miracle Algorithm

Entropy had swapped the charm and grace of his grandfather with the awkward pity of a conveyor belt of well-meaning bureaucrats. The paramedics, the police, the social worker, the temporary foster family. It had never occurred to him that he wouldn't be allowed to return to his home. Everyone had been kind. The sort of kindness that involved keeping themselves emotionally distant just in case he'd turned out to be a dick.

The funeral service had been small but tasteful. Gustavo's grandfather had passed into a better place, and then discreetly passed into the ground. Gustavo had taken the opportunity to dash off into the alleyways. Adults were easy to lose. He figured he still had a few more weeks to lean on grief as an excuse for poor behaviour. Longer if he was amenable the rest of the time. A few weeks was more than enough. He had a plan. He skittered down the ancient steps and wove through the tourists. German this time.

"Entschuldigung" he gasped on his way past, inducing a cluster of titters and smiles.

He pushed his key into the lock and moved into a much darker space than he had left. It had been both six days and a lifetime since he'd been in this room. Objects had been touched. Things had been picked up and returned in a manner that suggested a desire to obscure. Someone had been looking for something. He didn't imagine that paramedics and cops got paid much. He carefully entered his grandfather's room and checked the old man's keepsakes. Everything was still there. His old revolver, long since rusted beyond repair. Every single driver's license he'd ever owned. Gustavo breathed a sigh of relief and picked out the wedding rings of his mother and father. The combobulator had changed the way he thought about possessions. When you could have anything you wanted, the list of what you actually wanted tended to drop pretty quickly. But he would have been upset about the rings.

He shoved some food and a dog-eared copy of 'Your Combobulator and You' into what described itself as a 'Hergwurts, School of Witchcraft' backpack. The manual stressed that it was happy to be inspired by the physical crafting of an object but it drew the line at abusing trademarks. Gustavo found this baffling. The whole point of copyright was to make sure the creator received their payment for creative services rendered. If the machine was serving up product for free then it seemed a bit hypocritical to try to draw the ethical line in the sand here.

He switched into his favourite jacket and slung his backpack over his shoulder. It was time to put his plan into effect. The world might want to throw a barrage of well-meaning adults at him but with the combobulator he was all but unstoppable. The only thing standing in his way, he discovered moments later, was that the machine in question, was gone.

The screen door clashed shut and Ian appeared.

"Gustavo! Hey buddy, are you okay?"

He shrugged. Ian seemed okay but his default mode seemed to be set to 'patronise'. Gustavo wasn't sure if it was because he was just a kid or because he was a Portuguese kid.

Ian was white. Ian was British. Ian owned a pith helmet but he insisted that it was ironic.

"I understand this must be a rough time for you champ, but you can't run off like that. We've got people out looking for you."

Gustavo tried to look as pitiful as he could. It turned out not to be hard.

"Oh buddy," said Ian getting down onto one knee "You want a hug?"

His big dummy grin kept spreading across his face until it had nowhere left go. Gustavo shook his head 'no' then felt he should counter-offer. He held out his hand to shake. Ian sagely took his hand and it felt like it was done. Then Ian lunged forward.

"Let's meet half-way" he said pressing his shoulder to Gustavo's and patting him on the back. Gustavo's eyes widened like saucers. Didn't he realise how awkward this was? Were either of them getting what they wanted out of this situation? The discomfort continued and then suddenly Ian was upright again.

"Well, I'd better call off the cavalry."

Having proudly concluded his fatherly duty, he pulled out his phone and wandered into the kitchen. Gustavo collapsed onto the couch like he'd decided to emigrate there. For a while he simply gazed around the room. His focus alighting on unfamiliar items in the subconscious hope that something would make sense. The shadows from the window louvers climbed the walls. His backpack slipped from the couch to the floor and from it spilled the now useless manual. He picked it up and the invitation he'd forgotten all about slipped free.

handout.miracle.algorithm

With what little energy he had left he pulled himself out of the couch and slumped in front of the family PC. He typed in the three words but none of the results made sense. Why offer an invitation and not provide an address? He stared at the ceiling. You wouldn't. The address has to be on the card. He scoured the surface for hidden messages. He even whispered to the card to share its secrets. It remained static. So what if he assumed these three words WERE the address? He idly typed in 'three word address' into the search window and there it was. `https://what3words.com`

The globe partitioned out into ten billion squares. Each one with a unique three word name. He typed in handout.miracle.algorithm and held his breathe.

Nothing.

A three metre square in the middle of the ocean. He scrolled out. And scrolled, and scrolled. An empty patch of ocean on the other side of the planet. The disappointment and upset churned around inside him like a nest of rats. He tapped on satellite view and zoomed back in. The satellites couldn't even be bothered this far out to sea. The resolution was grainy. The compression artefacts showed a mosaic of dark and mid-blue tiles. He pressed his face close to the screen. One of those squares had an arrow pointing from each of its four sides.

There was a knocking at the front door and Gustavo lunged for the off button. He could hear Ian answer.

"How can I help you, officer?"

And Gustavo ran.

Interview

Detective Rafael Machado listened as the footsteps from the adobe cottage got louder. Panic made people predictable. Gustavo punched open the back door screen and became immediately snared in the long arms of Machado's law. Gustavo struggled, his eyes white.

"Gustavo I presume. You're not in trouble little guy. We just want to ask you a few questions."

This small tanned kid wearing dress pants and rolled up white sleeves. He'd only just returned from burying his last remaining family member. It might be worthwhile going gently. He loosened his grip and a change came over the boy. He stood up straight. A gentle smile filled up his face. He took a half step sideways in to where the light in the alleyway bounced off the red brick wall and an earthy tone warmed his cheeks.

"I'm happy to help you out, Sir. I'll do what I can."

He held his hands out, palms up. It was every checkbox ticked in the shyster's handbook. Rafael had worked with the fraud department for almost a decade now. His life had been a production line of charismatic grifters. This little bastard was gifted. A gifted grifter. He reaffirmed his grip.

"We're going to need you to come down to the station to answer a few questions."

"I've always wanted to visit a police station." he said and the way that he moved his head in the light made his eyes twinkle.

This fucking kid.

The boy stared around in fascination at the hubbub of the station. Most kids would. It was a scene out of a TV show. The romance that impressed them all was the same that had delighted Machado on his first day on the job all that time ago.

He stared at his notes but focused his attention to his peripheral vision. This allowed him to watch Gustavo without looking like he was watching him. It was a trick he'd spent a lot longer practising that he preferred to admit. Most children snuck bird-like glances at the guns. This kid was watching the exits.

"Is that a real gun?"

This kid.

"You got any ID?"

He dug in his pocket and pulling a small crisp card out. It read 'Gustavo Delgado. Your trash is my treasure'.

"You work in recycling?"

His trustworthy little face did its magic again.

"Yes, sir! I made money to help my grandpa out."

"I want to ask you about a device I found at your grandfather's house."

He watched a little air escape the boy's sails.

"I don't... uh"

Machado snatched up his letter opener and drove it point down at his desk. He'd used all his force and his knuckles were white. Gustavo's eyes went wide. The tip sat on the undamaged business card. Machado stabbed at it again and again and again.

"That's one hell of a business card, Master Delgado. It almost seems like it was made out of carbon nano-fibres. You must have a pretty amazing printer."

"You mean… the box?"

"Where did it come from?"

"Uh"

Another glance at the exit.

"I'm not screwing around here kid. This device is a matter of public safety. Where did it come from?"

He deflated.

"We found a machine… down at the river."

Machado started taking notes as Gustavo went through the whole saga stopping him occasionally to clarify.

"So the first machine created yours?"

"Yeah, it can make a copy of itself."

"So where's the original machine?"

"It was… taken."

"By who?"

"I… don't know. I didn't recognise them."

"Yes you did."

Machado dug into a folder on his desk and whipped out two photos of some recently acquired counterfeiters who were currently spending their time in lockup awaiting their day in court. Gustavo tried to hide the amusement in his face.

"That's them. What did they do?"

"We're talking to them about some very well made euros. Did you use the machine to make any money Gustavo?"

"I doubt that would have worked."

"Why's that?"

"It couldn't even get the brand name right on the Nintendos. Why would you ask for money anyway? The machine can give you whatever you want to buy."

In spite of himself Machado was starting to warm to the kid. He'd obviously decided that being helpful was to his benefit and now all that guile and talent was being used for good. Of course, he still didn't trust him as far as he could throw him.

Gustavo piped up, "So what did you make with the machine, when you first got it?"

Machado unlocked a desk drawer and reverently pulled out a Smith & Wesson Bodyguard 38. He placed it carefully between them.

"Have you tried it?" asked Gustavo.

"No. It's never been fired."

"It won't work. Not properly."

"How do you know."

"It says so in the manual."

"Where did you get a manual?"

He knew the answer even before he'd asked the question.

The machine was wrapped head to toe in a perfectly fitting white harness and locked to the wall. Gustavo's smaller machine had an identical wrapping and it gave the impression of a ghost mother and child.

"Just ask it for a manual of itself."

Machado slipped the key in and opened the lock. The straps and fabric fell away revealing the cornucopia device. He'd been worried when he found the second one and was relieved to discover that it had been fabricated in the first. Like a virus, if he could lock down the initial outbreak he could control it. It looked like he might be able to put the 'genie machine' back into the bottle.

Gustavo stepped forward and opened the door. There was nothing inside.

"Hey kid, leave that alone."

Something was wrong. He had something in his hand. A scrap of paper was flung into the machine and the door slammed shut. A moment later and the yellow star illuminated and pulsed.

"What did you do? What did you say to it?"

"I didn't say anything."

The boy grinned. The logo stopped pulsing. Machado pulled open the door and thousands of buzzing scarab beetles exploded from it. They climbed into the vents. They surged out the door into the hallways. Shouts of surprise erupted from his co-workers. Gustavo and Machado ran from the room covering their heads from the incessant swarm. The room was a madhouse. Bean sized creatures clattered against the walls as they urgently tried to find an exit. Windows were thrown open.

"No", yelled Machado, "Keep them contained!"

But it was too late. Like a flock of starlings the cloud of beetles plumed into the skies. Machado stared impotently from the window frame then rounded angrily on Gustavo. He was gone. He scanned the room but it was free of his wiry frame. The evidence lockup was also empty. He went to close the door of the machine and there at the bottom of the chamber was a small scrap of note paper. 'I would like 10000 flying discombobulator seeds'. A small tick appeared next to the spidery handwriting.

The genie was most definitely out of the bottle now.

That fucking kid.

Doctor Maya

Doctor Maya Gomez pulled up to the address that had been scrawled on the back of an old business card in near unreadable cursive. This was a barn. She stepped out into the churned up mud and skipped awkwardly between the driest patches. Dolce Vita heels had their place. This was not it. As the broken path coalesced she was able to approach the old barn with slightly more poise. A viscacha dashed across the unkempt lawn and into the wood pile. It was much more common for rats to populate this sort of farmland but she was sure it was a viscacha because if it was a rat she'd have already been back in her car. She stood in the door way and knocked on the wood.

"H.. hello?"

She took a cautious step and half a dozen lights popped on. It was not what she expected. The lighting hung low from the high ceilings. Each one a slightly different colour giving a warm festive tone to the leather couches and kitchenette. The space felt intimate.

"It's nice isn…"

She screamed.

"Oh my goodness. I'm so sorry. I'm Eduardo. We spoke on the phone."

His hands went up and back and he skipped a half step in retreat.

"Oh… you ah.. startled.." Maya mumbled as she turned away to obscure her blush.

"No. That was my fault. Lone city girl coming out into the country on a creepy undercover mission. I shouldn't have been so 'in my own head'. Probably scared seven bells out of you. You've got no reason to assume I'm not some pervert who's lured you out here under false pretences. That's not helping. Shouldn't have even brought it up. I'm not a pervert. Nope, shouldn't have said that either."

'Yes, I definitely wore the wrong shoes' thought Maya.

"You know what? How about I stop talking and just fill your order? Did you bring your order form?"

Maya's brain was using every available resource to quell her 'fight or flight' reflex and her mouth made a vague 'Huh' sound.

"The list? Of medications?"

"Oh yeah, right, sorry".

She dug a folded list from her bag and handed it to him.

"I'll have you sorted out in a moment. Take whatever you'd like from the kitchen. It's definitely not drugged. Haha! Nope. Sorry. Shouldn't have said that either."

He scurried out of the room shaking his head and muttering "nope nope nope" under his breath.

Maya tentatively opened the refrigerator to take a glance at the food she most definitely was not going to take a bite of. Rows and rows of salmon hors d'oeuvres. Mousse. Beer. Single serve wine. Pizza things. For a pervert he put on quite a spread.

"What is this place?" she muttered under her breath.

The flooring was lush carpet. The fittings were top notch. Enya was piping through a very, very nice sound system. This was a luxury experience in a venue you could describe generously as 'rustic' and less generously as 'fire-trap'.

"All done."

Eduardo wheeled out a trolley of boxes. The cardboard was smooth and tidy. Maya pulled her purse out of her handbag.

"Oh no" said Eduardo, "It's no charge. Call it an apology for my behaviour."

"What are you talking about? This is several thousands of dollars of product."

"It's fine. I can get more."

Parts of her brain screamed at her not to ask "Is it stolen?" but it still slipped out.

"No. It's absolutely not stolen. It's just… easy to get."

There was a moment they both stared at each other.

Finally Maya's brain kicked into gear, shut its mouth, took the trolley and left. The boxes were dumped into her backseat. The trolley left by the gate. She fell into the front seat and rested her head against the steering wheel. She jerked upright and stabbed at the lock door button, then rested her head again. This had been a very tense afternoon and she focused on a mindfulness technique to slow the thumping of her heartbeat. It was a trick that worked best when not being shocked bolt upright by a rapping on a driver's side window.

There was a rapping on the driver's side window.

Eduardo's face hung inches from hers.

"Hey! You're a smart lady. Do you know where I could get some sulphur?"

Maya peeled out onto the road as her adrenalin kicked in again, leaving startled viscachas scattered in her wake.

Gases and Particulates

Machado climbed the steps of the university building. The artificial scarabs had opened a real Pandora's box. While most of them scattered to the wind, one had taken up residence in front of the station. It burrowed into the pavement like a tick. Within hours the concrete had erupted into an angular stone boil. A cordon had been erected and by the morning a brand new vending machine sat gleaming in the sun. The officer on duty had explained that at some point it had kind of... unfolded. A gurney was summoned and it was locked up with the others.

'Only 9999 to go' Machado thought darkly as he knocked on the door of lab 115.

"Can I help you?" a light cautious voice bounced off the polished concrete floors.

"I'm Detective Machado, I'm looking for..." he started flipping page to page in his notebook.

"Oh, yes, sorry. Yes, we talked on the phone. I'm Vanessa. You're interested in... mapping air pollution?"

"Exactly. You study it here? You measure it?"

"Sure do. We've got instruments all over the city and surrounding areas. They suck in air and then we study the size and composition of the aerosols."

"What sort of aerosols?"

"You name it, we got it. Carbon-dioxide, carbon monoxide, nitrous oxide, sulfur dioxide, fine particles, ultra-fine particles, electrically charged particles, black carbon, organic carbon, pollen, volatile organic compounds, polycyclic aromatic hydrocarbons, cement dust, wood smoke."

"How about elements in the air? Helium? Water vapour?"

"For sure. We have an Aerosol mass spectrometer that detects the fingerprint of elements. It does light gasses like Helium but it also detects heavy metals and sodium…"

"Christ, heavy metals?"

"Oh yeah. We live in a city. There's still plenty of manufacturing going on here. Vehicle exhaust, smelting, painting. It opened my eyes to what I'm inhaling, I'll tell you that much. It's not nearly as bad as Lisbon though. Those cruise liners should be outlawed."

Machado sensed a rant and lunged to cut it off.

"Do you have a map of Porto since March? I suspect an air quality discrepancy at a particular location."

"Yes, I should be able to see that. Just let me load the data."

Vanessa tapped away at the keyboard, switching from window to window. App to App. It may as well have been arcane runes to Machado.

"So what are you after?" she asked. "Some company flaunting environmental laws?"

On the screen a map of Porto flashed up. The river cut west through the town. Each monitoring station indicated by a node and value. They speckled the map.

"There." Machado stabbed at the screen. "Can you show if pollution has dropped there in the last nine months?"

"Dropped?"

"That's right."

Vanessa scrubbed the dates backwards along the time line.

"Huh. That's weird."

"I can't make out what I'm looking at?"

"Let me switch to the city-wide heat map" she said.

The town was covered in a rainbow grid. Zoom, Pan. There was Gustavo's home. As the timeline swished left and right the patch above his home went from red to blue and back again.

"What's going on here? Is someone illegally filtering the air?"

"There's a machine there that's stripping the air of all its particulates. Now there are thousands of them out there and they've all been activated. Is there any way to check for this sort of change across the whole city?"

"What date range?"

"The last week."

"Oh, there's not really enough data in just a week. I might be able to give you something next week though."

"Is there any way you can speed that up? This could be a matter of national security."

"What is it you're looking for?"

Machado pulled out his phone.

"Thousands of these."

He revealed a photo of the Combobulator.

"Oh my god. Those are real?"

"You know what this is?"

"I saw it on the Internet this morning."

Vanessa switched windows and quickly tracked down the video in question. In it two teenagers in some sort of warehouse were laughing and grinning like idiots. The camera bounced around in the manner that had inspired the Internet cliché 'Kill the cameraman'. They were standing in front of the recognisable form of the Combobulator. Its door hung open.

"Nothing inside." stated teen one dramatically. Or at least, amateur dramatically.

He shut the door and, in a pale imitation of every second rate medium, asked for a 'Bucket Of Diamonds.' The door was flung open and a bucket of flawless gems was poured onto the ground in front of the camera. Machado had no doubt that they were real.

"There's a dozen of these." said Vanessa. "I thought it was some sort of viral marketing for a soft-drink company. Wait! Is it turning carbon in the atmosphere into diamonds?"

"And lord knows what else" muttered Machado as he made for the door.

"Tell me if you can find any other cold spots on that heat map. Until then, I've got a missing person to find."

Homelessness

The first night on the streets had been cold and uncomfortable. Gustavo's funeral clothes, stiff and scratchy as they were, were at least warmer than his usual t-shirt and pants. He'd barely slept. The machines were out there now. All he had to do was find one, feed it, and he could get away from all of this. It was time for him to grow up. To become his own man. These were comforting fantasies as tears ran down his face in the shadows of the garden he'd taken refuge in. He missed his home. He missed his grandpa. He missed being looked after. He did not miss Ian.

The next morning he was on the prowl, strolling with intent up and down the main thoroughfares. There were ten thousand Combobulators out there waiting to give everyone exactly what they wanted. He wasn't sure what sort of hell was going to break loose when they worked out what that was but he thought it prudent to be out of town by the time that happened. The city was starting to wake up. Store owners swept debris back and forth between their own store front and their neighbours. Tour guides were tidying up their boats for a day of 'peace and calm' breaking.

There it was. Standing discreetly on the side of the square. Early morning commuters wandering past like it wasn't the most amazing device in the world. He trudged past it, head down, carefully watching his peripheral. Nothing. On his third pass he sauntered up to the box and asked for a warm jacket, a tent and a box of breakfast bars. The machine's insignia warmed to life and moments later an error appeared.

'Breakfast bars require, sulfur, potassium, magnesium…'

A dozen ingredients scrolled across the display before finally the machine asked to 'Continue anyway?'.

"Continue" said Gustavo. The crest dulled, a click sounded. He opened the machine and slipped into the jacket. It fit perfectly. The tent was light and strong. It had a strap that Gustavo slipped over his shoulder. He was still hungry but at least he had somewhere to sleep tonight. He considered loading the machine with refuse from a bin but it felt so exposed here. What he really needed was a Combobulator to himself again.

"Oh yeah" he muttered to himself.

"Can I please have a Combobulator seed with a toggle set to off?"

The machine happily complied and a moment later he was scurrying through the alleyways of Porto with salvation in his pocket. His stomach growled. He didn't know how long the new machine would take to form and even then he would need to find a dozen elements before he could rely on it for food. It couldn't spit out money. He considered making some diamonds to sell but that detective was on the ball. An eleven year old hocking diamonds wasn't the most covert of activities.

As he wandered down to the river he idly picked up discarded trash. A half eaten sandwich here. An unfinished soft drink. The best place to get the elements of food was food itself. The machine was going to break it down first anyway. There was no reason to be concerned with germs at that point. An hour later and the pockets of his new jacket were full of trash. He was wandering down towards the river mouth. He needed a safe place to lay up. The boat house where they'd hidden the original machine had been perfect but it had become exposed.

He ambled up behind the train station. The houses here would be classed as 'shabby unchic'. One yard in particular was especially overgrown. Gustavo skipped over the low wall and ducked past the windows. The backyard was even worse. Long tails of whip-grass filled the space. A garden shed squatted in the back corner.

Perfect.

The door pealed open and age-old cobwebs fluttered from the frame. A dusty floor. Concrete brick walls. He sealed himself in and pulled out the seed. The scarab was smaller than his thumb. As he turned it, the light scattered upon its surface and gave off iridescent rainbows. The toggle on its belly matched the overall design of the device. How did it know how to do that? He flipped the switch and the bug started to struggle. He cast it onto the floor. Tiny wings unfurled and it buzzed into the air. For a moment it seemed it was trying to escape the confines of the shed but it settled into the corner and burrowed into the soil.

Gustavo waited for something to happen. It didn't. After a few more minutes it didn't again. His sleepless night was starting to pound his head with waves of fatigue. He unfurled the tent onto the floor. A high pitched drone began and to his surprise the whole tent started to inflate. Struts along the edge shot out like an extra skinny balloon. The top spine was last to charge and a simple, safe space had appeared. He gripped the inflated struts and they were stiff as steel. He climbed inside. The floor was soft. He'd slept on inflated furniture before and it was torturous. This was firmer. Supportive. There was even a little pillow. He wouldn't lay here long. 'Just enough to...'. His body took over and plunged him into a cosy and deserved sleep.

He awoke to a dry mouth and an unignorable hunger. The tent blocked almost all the light and when he climbed out it was into the late afternoon sun streaming in via the cracks in the walls. He turned and there stood the machine. It had fabricated itself while he dreamed and was now ready to go.

"Water please" croaked Gustavo.

'Calcium, magnesium, potassium' crawled across the face of the beast.

Gustavo dug into his pockets and threw his trash into the shelf of the machine. The display went quiet and when he asked again a water bottle presented itself without complaint. He guzzled it greedily then used the machine to finally relieve his hunger. Those food scraps wouldn't last long. He winced at having to start a whole new list of elements. The first thing he needed was all the elements that food need to grow. Plants made it look so easy. Most of what they needed they just plucked out of the air which the machine would happily do. The rest they would just draw up out of the soil. He looked at his feet, then around at the fast darkening garden shed. He grabbed a half full sack of fertiliser and dropped it into the machine.

It was generally fairly quiet as it imbibed material but Gustavo imaged that he heard a sigh of contentment. It was a moment before he realised that he himself was making that sound. He had food. He had water. He had shelter. Now he needed a plan.

"Please give me a pencil and notebook" he asked the Combobulator.

A warm thrum and Gustavo had everything he needed. He was going to Handout Miracle Algorithm.

Day Off

Matthias sipped on his rooibos as he leafed through the month's accounts. Cotton prices were up again and he'd finally recovered from all that warlord nastiness from a few years ago. In his mind's eye there was a BMW 5 Series waiting to engulf him in her comforts. The phone rang. It was a number he didn't recognise.

"Matthias Akombi"

"Mister Matthias sir?"

"Speaking"

"It's Cesar sir. From the plantation. How are you today sir?"

"What... What's wrong?"

"Oh nothing is wrong today Mr Matthias. It is a great day. I just wanted to give you a call to tell you I won't be in today."

"You don't sound very sick to me Cesar."

"On the contrary sir. I feel better than I have in my entire life. And I realised I'd hate to waste this day picking cotton and fixing farm machinery."

There was background laughing.

"Is this some sort of joke? Who else is there?"

"Oh it is just the dog laughing sir."

More chuckling.

"This is absolutely unacceptable Cesar. Get yourself down to the plantation, NOW!"

"No thank you, Mr Matthias."

"I can't believe what I'm hearing. I give you this

opportunity. There are plenty of people starving who'd be happy to take your position."

"My position?"

"Your job is on the line here you lazy Kadjidi! Do you understand me?"

"Oh, I see. And if I don't turn up today you will give my job to someone else?"

"Damn straight. And just for this insolence I'm docking you a day's pay."

"That seems fair, Mister Matthias. Please accept my humblest apologies."

"I should expect so. Honestly I don't know what's come over you."

"I have one more thing to say Mister Matthias."

"It's alright Cesar. You can apologise by putting in more hours tonight."

"It's not that Mister Matthias. I just wanted to tell you that I WON'T BE IN TOMORROW EITHER!"

His big booming laugh was joined by a chorus of laughter behind him before the phone went 'pip' and was silent again.

Matthias had seen this before. You worked people hard and occasionally they went off the deep end. It would be a shame to loose Cesar though. He had a good head for engines. But when his belly was empty and he came crawling back he'd be damned if he gave him a second chance. You lost respect and then where were you? Anyway, there were plenty of desperates to choose from. With half of Chad literally starving to death it didn't take much to motivate them.

The phone rang.

"Mister Matthias sir. It's Ahmad."

"Ahmad. Just the person. I've had to let Cesar go."

"That's a real blow sir. He was always so good with engines."

"No matter. I'll need you to find someone to replace him."

"Today sir?"

"As soon as possible Ahmad. Those trucks won't fix themselves."

"Sorry sir, that won't be possible. I was just calling to tell you that I WON'T BE IN TODAY EITHER!"

Boisterous laughter cackled down the phone line and Matthias stared at it in astonishment. It was in this moment (though he could never know it) that the brand new BMW 5 Series that was destined to be his slipped from his grasp.

Ship's Birth

Machado stood in the park looking out over the river mouth with his phone held to his ear. He covered his other ear as one of the city's trams squealed into the terminus behind him.

"Okay, thank you Vanessa."

The pollution data hadn't been much use in the end. There were so many machines that once people worked out how to use them whole patches of the sky started to heal. The first cold spot though (aside from Gustavo's flat), was down here at the tram terminus. Vanessa admitted that it could just be an outlier reading but Machado could feel it in his bones.

He'd become obsessed. He could at least see this in himself. But something big was happening. Already there were all sorts of societal problems cropping up. Pawn shops had all shut pending. Pending what? People could get whatever they wanted for free now. The only scarcity was the machines themselves and people were already starting to work out that they could just get the machine to birth a smaller version of itself.

Porto had been flooded with diamonds. Machado knew that the diamond trade was intentionally limiting the supply to drive up prices. He doubted they had anything like the stockpile that Porto now had. Stories were also coming out of Chad and Uruguay. The fantasy of having a machine deliver anything you wanted was like catnip on social media and new videos were constantly filtering to the top of the algorithm. Soon, someone was going to try printing the manual. Then they'd find the scarab trick. In a week the whole country would be filled with them. And it was all because of Gustavo.

He'd been strolling around this area for a week looking for any sign. That smart kid might try to cover his tracks but he was going to slip up eventually. A group of lithe joggers bounced past. A vagrant pushed a shopping trolley along the concrete. School children jostled each other and squealed in a manner that made childless couples just a little bit self-satisfied.

Machado scanned them looking for that one disarming face that had been haunting his waking moments. Nothing. And what was he going to do when he found him? Gustavo hadn't done anything illegal. The country was in chaos and his little hands were clean. At least he could make sure he was safe. It was his fault that the boy hadn't returned to his foster home. Gustavo might be the thorn in his side but he also felt some responsibility for him.

The joggers had made their way to the surf beach. The vagrant had disappeared. Machado was alone under the palms. The tour boats arced across the river to make their way back under the famous bridges. A sailboat caught his eye. Passersby had started to gather. Was it capsizing? The mast was at a rakish angle. The hull seemed to point into the air. He started to stride towards it to try to get a better view. The mast slowly lifted. The bow stretched and firmed. A cabin started to rise from the centre, like a piece of origami… UNFOLDING! He started to sprint. The vagrant stood on the boat ramp with a supermarket trolley sitting empty on its side. A droning sound was coming from the 14 metre long sailboat.

"Hey! HEY!"

A bearded face lifted in shock. He was holding the boat by a single rope. With all the suppleness of an eleven year old boy this bedraggled figure leapt for the vessel. It had not completed its expanding process and wobbled and distorted under his weight. Now untethered, the boat started to drift away into the deeper water. Machado realised it was escaping him and changed direction towards the tidal gauge that sat on the out-jutting groin.

"Gustavo!"

The vagrant pulled off his disguise.

"Gustavo! You're not in trouble!" Machado lied.

Looking down, he could see the deck firming up. Gustavo scurried to the helm and began to toy with the controls. A light whirring began and the electric motors aligned the boat up with the centre of the river. Machado tried to weigh his options. It was a fool's game to try to jump down to the boat. It would be a simple enough process to just radio the coast guard and have them intercept. His instincts kicked in and instead he was suddenly in the air. He clattered to the deck and it was only through luck that he didn't roll his left ankle. His right ankle did not fair so well.

Ribbons of pain spiralled up his body. His vision did a quick reset through every colour of the rainbow. Once it was complete he lifted his head to see Gustavo dash below deck. The motors hummed and sails started to unfurl. He limped to the cabin door, past the helm console that flashed 'Auto-pilot'.

As he climbed into the dim cabin space his eyes, still recalibrating from his graceless landing, once again found themselves pushed to their limits. In the gloom he could just make out Gustavo reaching up to an emergency handle on the hull. In his other hand was a gas mask. His brain tried to join the dots but there were too many extra dots. Gustavo yanked the handle and there was a whooshing that shocked them both. The boy tried to lift the mask to his face but his pupils rolled back in his face and he slumped to his side.

'Ha! Dummy!' thought Machado as he too collapsed to the floor.

Above him the main sail unfurled and the boat made for the ocean.

Spain

'The commercial traffic was thick in both directions on the main road between Porto and Madrid. Almost all freight into Spain was coming from Portugal. Most of the professional drivers had suddenly found their local jobs drying up but Spaniards wanted cheap, high quality products and the Portugese truckers were perfectly placed to provide them.'

Tiago Souza set the document aside as the Spanish Minister of Foreign Affairs was led into his office.

"Mister Michael Almus for you Mister Souza."

"Thank you, Adriana."

Michael Almus was tall and tanned. He looked more like a tennis player than a member of government. Usually he looked like he was winning the match.

"Michael. Good to see you in the flesh again."

"Yes, well" stammered Micheal, "This is a somewhat delicate matter."

Tiago suppressed a grin. It was nice to have the shoe on the other foot for a change.

"Anything I can get for you? And I do mean… anything." he tried to smile graciously but it ended up coming out as mischief.

"Yes, well. Tiago. You've come straight to the heart of the problem. We need to discuss this fabricator issue. There are thousands of tonnes of high quality product flooding our markets. As you can expect our manufacturing industries are struggling. This huge influx of cheap products has wiped out so many businesses. Unemployment has sky-rocketed along with crime. It's like we woke up one morning and China had moved in next door."

"I feel like I woke up and China and Saudi Arabia left me a baby that I had to raise."

"OH, I'm weeping for you Tiago. Such a tragedy. Free fuel, and super-materials that you can sell to the world. It must keep you up at night."

"You mock, but at least your problems have precedence. Our economy has completely tanked. Over 50% of our population is no longer paying any tax. I've got treasury working on scenarios."

"Yes, but it does help that you've got access to infinite resources I suspect."

"It certainly takes some of the sting out of it."

Almus banged the table.

"How can you be so cavalier? If this isn't managed properly it could be the end of capitalism as we know it."

"Why would we need capitalism if everyone has what they needed to prosper? If we play our cards right this could be the beginning of a Utopian age."

"Easy to say when you have all the cards. This is unfair competition. You agreed to be part of the union. You need to share this technology."

"Obviously you know that's impossible. Whenever a machine crosses into Spain it deactivates. Look, we want to help you Micheal. There's no point living like kings here when it's so easy for a revolution to occur next door. You know what they do to kings during the revolution, right?"

"We want tariffs."

"I don't think that's a great idea. Tariffs that could balance this out would be so large that you end up incentivising smuggling. No, We've got a better idea. We want to keep our neighbours safe, so I've been given authorisation to offer a trade."

Tiago Souza pulled out a map of the Iberian Peninsula and ran his finger down the line between the two countries.

"We'd like to offer you two square kilometres on the edge of our border. There's already a warehouse filled with fully operating machines. You want access to these machines we want to give them to you."

Almus furrowed his brow.

"And what do you want in return?"

"No tariffs. No extra taxes on your raw materials."

"Seems fair."

"Also, We want an enclave. Here! In Aldehuela."

He pointed to a spot 30 kilometres from the centre of Madrid.

"An enclave? What? Why?"

"We believe that the value of land we're giving you should be equal to the value of land you're giving us."

"No. This is ridiculous. We're not giving up sovereign land so close to the capital."

"Okay then. I guess we'll start the process of debating tariff amounts. I've got a proposal here for you to read through. Could you just sign this first though?"

"What's this?"

"It's a statement showing that I offered you Utopia and you refused it based on some sort of patriotic ideals."

Infuriation coloured Micheal's face.

"I'm… not signing that." he spat.

Tiago beamed a huge smile and clapped his hands together.

"Oh, that's wonderful to hear."

Water

Gustavo's eyes fluttered open. His head was throbbing and his stomach felt like the floor was shifting. Lights danced in front of his eyes. Important diagnostic information regarding his situation hit his brain in a torrent. Once the initial reports came in, the sensations began to settle down. Hard carpet. The floor continued to sway. The lights were still dancing.

He was all at sea.

He clambered up and peered out the porthole. Waves and clouds skipped past but reference points were unsettlingly absent. He grabbed a diamond glass from the kitchenette and emptied it of water twice over. Gustavo didn't realise how delicious water could taste. Electrical motors hummed as the solar powered desalinator started to refill the water stores. He gagged and then returned a good portion of the water he'd imbibed into the sink. His stomach was playing a rhumba beat.

He headed aft towards the console only to find his way blocked by the collapsed form of Detective Machado. Gustavo was the captain of this vessel. He needed to be commanding and in control. He gave himself permission to freak out, which he did for several minutes pausing only briefly multiple times to assure himself that he had himself under control now. He washed his face and tried to work out what the hell he was going to do.

The ship's combobulator tickered a simple message across its front panel. 'Invalid Location'. They were in international waters. He quietly opened the machine and inside was a small collection of prepackaged meals he'd requested in the moments before Detective Machado had burst through the door. The machine was collecting water from outside the boat to craft into basic foodstuffs but it would have stopped the moment they left Portuguese waters. No matter. He couldn't have gone too far. He'd just turn around.

He drummed his fingers and peeked sideways at the detective. He was stalling. He knew he had to check for a pulse. Oh no, what if he'd killed a policeman. What remained of his rational brain tried to recall whether throwing a policeman's body into the sea counted as piracy. The rest of his brain tried to stop itself from silently screaming.

He knelt down and carefully touched his fingers to the nape of the man's neck. Nothing. Was he doing this properly? Was it only on one side? Machado suddenly gasped and adjusted himself before returning to a deep sleep. Gustavo could feel a pulse now. It was his own and it threatened to erupt from his chest.

He tip-toed past and unlocked the boat's console. The touchscreen lit up to show the boat's current position. Santa Cruz. Gustavo boggled. How had they travelled almost 1300 kilometres? Average speed… 19 kph. He looked around at the boat as it juggled the sails and tiller. The wake was smooth and flat as a billion bubbles jostled to the surface. He tapped another option on the flat panel. 72.6 hours since launch.

Three days.

If that detective wasn't dead yet he couldn't be far off. He unclipped the storage panel with a big red cross on it and found some bags of saline and an IV needle. It was huge. Gustavo stared at it with his eyes wide. He could do this. People do this every day. Diabetics do it to themselves. All he had to do was stop crying and it'd be easy. One two three, done.

A meaty palm grabbed his shoulder and he was suddenly looking into the horrific gaunt face of Detective Machado.

"OH thank god!" whispered Gustavo.

"Water!" croaked the detective before dropping to his knees.

Gustavo returned momentarily with a glass of water.

"Sip it!" he ordered, but Machado sucked it back as quickly as he could.

A moment later half of it was oozing across the deck.

"You're dehydrated. You've got to sip it a little at a time."

Machado swayed as the boat traversed the cross swell. Tiny bird-like sips seemed to bring colour back into his cheeks. Gustavo rummaged through the first aid kit and pulled out something labelled 'Oral Hydration Therapy'. When he'd asked the machine for a boat he'd planned out as much as he could and written it all down on sheets of paper. He'd labelled this section as 'first aid' but hadn't given it any idea about requirements. He didn't know how smart the machines were but he was glad this one was smart enough to stock itself.

He tapped a few buttons on the console and a shade cloth climbed out across the deck putting them both into shadow. They sipped quietly on their solutions.

"What happened?" asked Machado after a few minutes.

"I had a knockout gas just in case I was boarded by pirates."

"Knockout gas? Like in a comic book?"

"I expected to have more time to deploy it and I didn't get my mask on in time."

"How long was I out?"

Quietly Gustavo replied "It's Thursday"

"What happens Thursday?" asked Machado.

Gustavo cocked his head, "Today. Today happens."

Machado looked like he was doing Sudoku's in his head.

"THREE DAYS?! Where the hell are we?"

He leapt to his feet and scanned the horizon as it wobbled and rapidly tilted from horizontal to vertical. Machado had passed out again. Gustavo tried to move him but he was too heavy, so he grabbed some bedding from the cabin and tried to make him as comfortable as possible.

This had all gone wrong. There wasn't enough food. Machado was going to force him to turn the boat around and, let's face it, probably arrest him. He certainly wasn't going to get another chance to make this trip.

The boat ploughed on through the waves, nimbly skipping through the white caps. It piloted itself and seemed more than capable of keeping them on route. Machado couldn't take control of the boat himself but he could definitely force Gustavo to unlock it for him. His eyes twinkled. 'Unless I lock myself out'.

Dining

Officer Joao Otero strolled past the Plaza Matriz. He'd been doing this job for decades and he'd never felt the square so at ease. It had become absurdly relaxing since the machines arrived. Montevideo was generally pretty safe but it turned out that when no-one was desperate for basic services, lawlessness dropped to levels that a less patient man would call boring. He plodded a policeman's tempo with his feet. Many of the shops had 'for rent' signs pasted on them. It was hard to sell people on the trappings of commerce when they could get them for free from their in-house cornucopia.

The Chanel store was still open. He found that so strange. The machines could give you a bag that was flawless and robust, but they'd never match the branding. You could ask for a Louis Vuitton and end up with a Louisse Buttons. Same (or better) quality and yet people who still had jobs were lining up to grab them.

Now that 'goods' had been taken out of the 'goods and services' equation, money had been going through a strange dance back and forth. People with service jobs suddenly had an influx in wealth as their expenditure on purchases dropped to zero. Salespeople were put out of work in droves. Rent wasn't being made. Evictions began. Tent cities started to crop up on the outskirts of town. Nice tent cities. Clean water. Plenty of food. High quality temporary lodging. The only thing these people needed was land.

Of course this meant that half of the population couldn't

afford services. Tour guides. Theme parks. Cinemas. Income for non-vital services dropped. But at the same time so did running costs. People didn't need jobs so the wages had to increase to lure them in. No one was working out of desperation anymore. People worked because they wanted to be able to afford the things that the machine couldn't provide.

Everyone was trying to figure out how to adjust to this new normal. With fewer people paying tax Otero didn't think the city could afford a large police presence. Most of his day now was helping tourists with directions. He wondered how long he had. But then, he'd been doing this a long time. He owned his own home. Had everything a man could want. He could retire tomorrow. But then he wouldn't be "Officer Otero".

"Good morning Joao"

He looked up to see Pedrina's shining face. The early morning light did helter-skelters through the ringlets in her hair.

"Pedrina. Another rosy day on the Plaza."

"It never stops" she said popping open another cafe chair.

"How's business?"

"Oh very well. And you Joao?"

He stopped.

"No, Pedrina. I really want to know. So many of these little places have closed up shop. How do you even manage when people can ask for whatever they want from a device in their home?"

"It hasn't been so bad. People need a social space. Tourism is way up. And running costs are way down." she said wryly.

They both chuckled and she continued.

"The experience of a restaurant isn't just the ingredients in the food. My chefs have been let off the leash and can now try out all the recipes they've never been able to. Great cooking isn't just about instinct. It's experimentation. Osan and Todd have been like kids in a candy store. They want to find out the best way to cook Waghu beef? They experiment with a dozen cuts. Anything that goes wrong goes back into the machine and there's no wastage."

"Astounding"

"If you don't have talent in your kitchen then you're in a race to the bottom. But cooking is an art, and art still has value. The machine can't create that. It can only duplicate someone else's."

"But these new prices. You must be struggling with rent."

"Oh, I've renegotiated my rent. Look around. I could have my pick of any of these places. The cost to refurbish is minimal now. I've got my landlord right where I want him."

Joao put his hat back on.

"I'm coming back at lunchtime."

"I'll open a bottle of my finest for you, Officer Joao."

"Oh Pedrina. If I was 10 years younger..." he let the moment hang in the air, "I would still be way, WAY too old for you."

Her bright easy laugh flashed across the plaza tiles.

No Turning Back

Machado's stomach churned. It felt like his mouth was filled with cobwebs. Dreams of spilled milkshakes slowly resolved into the splash of waves against the hull. He stared up at the boat's wheel and some sort of marquee had been stretched across the deck shading him from the sub-tropical sunlight.

Having learned from his mistakes he lay very, very still and did a stock-take of his situation. Number one. He smelt. A rinse and some toothpaste would surely help him right himself. Number two. Rehydration. His body was sending him signals that were impossible to defer. Number three. Turn this boat around.

He'd dealt with run-aways before. Grade-school kids who'd had their first argument with their parents holed up in a park play set with a backpack full of sandwiches. Teens with a stolen credit card getting broken sleep at the train station. Gustavo was on a whole new level. He wondered if this situation was playing out all over Portugal as disenfranchised children suddenly got access to all the resources needed to survive. A lot of angry men were going to wake up alone in the forthcoming months.

He made his way to his feet. It took a moment before the boat stopped floating around underneath him. It was very stable. Some water splashed on his face and some bathroom business took place. His body lightly trembled but the savage chills from earlier had sopped up the rehydration fluid and started to transport electrolytes to where they were needed most.

Gustavo sat on the bow of the vessel sipping from a juice tetrapack. He wore big sunglasses perched on his head and a lurid tropical shirt. The pair of binoculars he scanned the horizon with seemed comically large. The parody of a vacationer. Machado found what Gustavo was watching. The only land they could see. He assumed the shoreline of Portugal but a glimpse at the computer panel next to the wheel indicated… the Canary Islands? They were a long way from the park play set. He tapped on the interface and the message 'Hello Gustavo. Press fingerprint to unlock' blinked onto the screen. Machado pressed his thumb to the screen and, unsurprisingly it returned 'Unrecognised fingerprint.'

"Gustavo!"

The boy started but then climbed to his feet and made his way back to the deck. He was trying to play it cool, and for an eleven-year old he was doing a pretty good job. This kid.

"Young Master Delgado. It is time for our little expedition to come to its conclusion. I'm sure your foster parents are wondering…" he stared around at the mostly open sea, "what country's coastline you're navigating."

Gustavo steeled himself.

"Detective Machado. Please don't get angry… but we can't go back."

"And why's that?"

"Because I locked the computer."

"Then unlock it."

Gustavo pressed his thumb against the screen.

Unrecognised fingerprint.

Then his index finger.

Unrecognised fingerprint.

Each finger successively failed. Machado went red.

"Stop playing around and turn this damned boat around."

"You weren't supposed to be here Detective and I'm sorry,

but I knew you'd want me to turn the boat around so I removed all my fingerprints from the system. It's a one way trip and we can't stop it."

Machado went white and jabbed at the interface.

Unrecognised fingerprint.

He tugged at the wheel but it spun freely having no effect on their course. The sails collected the wind. The rudder took orders from its computerised master. If he could cut the ropes perhaps he could steer them in to one of the nearby islands.

"I need a knife" he muttered as he dashed into the kitchenette.

Drawers were yanked open and slammed shut. The shimmering clash of utensils trilled out again and again.

"Where are the bloody knives?!"

"I threw them all overboard."

He roared from inside the cabin and then, a moment later Machado emerged with a butter knife and started sawing at the rigging.

"It's woven nano-fibre Detective. You can't cut it."

Raphael Machado collapsed defeated. He'd over-exerted himself again and his vision started to swim. Head between knees he tried to regulate his breathing. The gurgle in his inner ear retreated and he gathered up his anger and put it away.

"If we're stuck on a one-way trip, what, pray tell, is the terminus?"

Gustavo bit his bottom lip. He looked like he was trying to decide something. From his pocket he pulled a card. 'You have been cordially invited to handout.miracle.algorythym.'

"And what is at handout.miracle.algorythym?"

Gustavo slipped his sunglasses on and stared out across the foredeck.

"Answers"

District Porto

Katie inched her company car across the muddy parking lot. The swarms of eager "shoppers" had not yet filled the yards to capacity. She had moved to Madrid a few scarce weeks before the economy went south. High quality goods poured in through the western borders and her new position as an aid to the foreign affairs mister went from challenging to overwhelming almost overnight.

There had been a big song and dance by the powers that be when the land swap had occurred. Spain would get its borders expanded to include the nano-fabrication facilities that had already been built. Portugal would get a small allotment of drainage and farmland on the outskirts of Spain's capital. For two weeks the main road to Spain's new sliver of Combobulator-friendly real estate was thick with trucks moving raw materials out and bringing fabricated goods back. Then overnight. It stopped. The machines wouldn't work. The display registered only 'Invalid Country Code'.

At the same time District Porto had erupted in the enclave. Heavy machinery had tamped down the loamy soil. Dusty roads fed what looked like a cluster of sporting fields. The day the machines at the border went silent the work here began in earnest. Portugal had pulled out all stops to get their structures up. Roads were paved. Signs erected. In all, it had taken three days for the first structure to be up and running. Onlookers described the massive sun shades 'congealing' into place.

The gates had opened and the public had poured in. The magical machines happily hummed to themselves like they were drawing power from the newly claimed soils of Portugal itself. Even now with the sun just cresting the horizon, the rows and rows of sheds were beginning to fill with enthusiastic shoppers. Crates of prepackaged foods were wheeled away on trolleys. Giddy teenagers precariously balanced big screen TVs between them.

Katie peered around for the deep red suit she had been assured would be present and the already grinning face of Tiago Souza poking out the top of it.

"Katherine! Over here" he called out as he undid the lid of a box of what revealed themselves to be Portuguese tarts.

She rankled at the informality of it. Why was it that women in politics never got the respect of being called by their surname?

"Mr Souza. You've come a long way."

"Tiago, please. And I come bearing gifts. Do you mind if I call you Katherine?"

For a moment she considered a pointed comment but a lifetime of social conditioning had her reply…

"My friends call me Katie."

She instantly hated herself.

"Katie, I want you to try one of these tarts. The machines make them taste just like the ones my grandmother would make."

The early morning sun warmed his cheeks and his eyes twinkled. She'd been warned about this. Tiago Souza had weaponised a disarming nature. Here he stood in a ridiculous suit offering bakery treats while discussing his family. She ignored his cakes and rounded on the market place. Girders like tree trunks thrust up into the air and tasteful shades spread out across the area. Speckled amongst the rows of machines were bathrooms and playparks. On her first visit she'd had the impression of an outdoor casino floor. The vending machines just needed to rattle off irritating jingles to complete the illusion.

"You knew this would happen didn't you, Mr Souza?"

"I was, quietly confident, yes."

He took a bite of a tart. They did smell quite good. No matter what you thought of the salted cod and the sardines, the Portugese could pull off a mean custard tart.

"What's your end game here?"

He chuckled.

"End Game? You make it sound like a nefarious scheme. Portugal has made sure that our neighbours get access to the same boons that have blessed us. We've set up a venue that allows your citizens and your businesses access to every product they could ever imagine. Your country is in a position where it can rely on stable access to anything it cares to imagine. Including..."

He waggled the lid of the box again. Katie's stomach begged her to take one but she needed to show resolve. She wasn't about to play into Portugal's hands just yet. Her hand, however had no such political motivations and she was momentarily surprised to have a mouthful of pastry. It did taste very good.

"And what happens next, Mr Souza?"

"Indeed this is what I wanted to discuss with you. Looking out over District Porto I feel like this has been a wonderful trial run. Your citizens seem truly delighted. In my home country we've found mental health is at an all time high and it would appear the same results are showing up here."

"When people don't have to worry about where their next meal comes from it does seem to benefit their mind set."

"With that in mind, Portugal has decided to relinquish control of the enclave back to Spain."

"WHAT?"

"Effective immediately District Porto will revert back to the ownership of Felipe the sixth, King of Spain."

Katie stared around at the thousands of machines in horror.

"But the machines… They'll shut down."

Tiago brushed crumbs off his chin.

"I expect so, yes."

"You can't. There will be riots. The social discord…"

She could barely speak as the implications collapsed on her.

"Well, we do have an option that would allow your citizens to enjoy the delights of Portugal."

Katie rounded on him, her face bewildered.

Tiago's face broke into an even larger grin.

"Unconditional Surrender."

The taste of tart turned to ash in her mouth.

Fishing

'Fishing,' pondered Machado, 'was supposed to be a relaxing pursuit'. Typically it was not done at speed. The vessel sliced through the water like a pair of sharp scissors through wrapping paper. From what he could tell, the boat was up on foils. You couldn't feel the waves slapping against the side until the chop got high. He reeled in his lure and the sinker bounced along the hull.

They needed food. The boat had inbuilt desalination and happily used nanotech to fill its stores as they left Portuguese waters but there were only enough muesli bars and cordial for one. Never trust a child to stock a larder. If he was going to be trapped on a transatlantic prison boat he was damn well going to have some meat. Gustavo claimed he'd planned to create a more diverse menu on the voyage out and blamed Machado for their predicament. 'Sure' he thought, flicking the lure as far ahead as he could throw, 'He was the bad guy'.

Gustavo sat at the… front? Bow? .. FORE! Machado was slowly absorbing the lingua-franca of the sea. The boy stared through his binoculars with his legs hanging through the lifelines.

"Hey! Don't slip through there. I'm not turning this boat around if you fall out."

Gustavo barely reacted. He'd retracted into himself and Machado couldn't blame him. Even he had to admit his anger had got the best of him. Trapped on an insane voyage with the tiny scam artist that had dropped all of Portugal into chaos. It had taken him days to accept his fate. In that time he'd called the boy a lot of things that he wasn't proud of. At his lowest point he'd tried to bite through the ropes that were guiding them over the foamy crests. Nothing could stop this wild, though eerily comfortable, ride.

He reeled in again and cast his line to the… he paused. (port and left have four letters…) starboard side. This damned street urchin had probably doomed them to starvation. And what would they do if they made it to the South Pacific and nothing was there. Marooned in the middle of the sea. Their only hope would be to catch the eye of…

That was a sparkle on the horizon. A speedboat? They had only seen a handful of cargo vessels in the time they'd been out here.

"Gustavo! Eight O'clock."

As Gustavo got a closer look, Machado dared to entertain the notion of rescue. If he could just get their attention. This might be the one chance they have. A pleasure cruiser this far off the West African coastline?

"They're heading towards us." called Gustavo.

Decades of experience tugged gently at the knot of Machado's hope.

"Are they… carrying anything?" he held his breath.

"It looks like they're holding up fishing rods?"

Machado scurried along the lifelines to the bow and impatiently snapped his fingers.

"I can do it" said Gustavo defiantly.

"GIVE ME THE BINOCULARS!"

A thundercloud descended on Gustavo's face and he churlishly handed them over. Machado peered through them. The horizon bounced around and then his stomach and heart followed suit. Machine guns.

"Pirates!" he muttered under his breath. "Of course it's pirates."

Gustavo's eye went wide.

"Cooool".

"No, not cool. Very not cool. These aren't swash-buckley pirates. These are 'shoot you in the head and steal your boat' pirates. Though admittedly," he continued "so were the swash-buckley ones".

He raced below deck and emerged moments later with his pistol.

"Gustavo, you need to hide. Now!"

"I can help."

"You can help, by hiding."

The speedboat drew along the… (four letters) port side of their boat. The roar of the twin engines was a shock after more than a week of quiet sailing. Four gunmen and a driver. They yelled out in a foreign language and drew their fingers across their throats. Machado tried his best to look non-threatening.

"I can't stop it." he called out.

He knew they wouldn't be able to understand him even if they could hear him so he tried to mime helplessness, firstly by miming a steering wheel and then shrugging. If the pursuers had deciphered his message they responded by ignoring it. Machine guns were pointedly pointed. Their mime, he considered, was more effective than his. If he could just take out the driver, then perhaps they could gain a few moments of advantage. But then what? Well then he'd have had a few moments to come up with the next step of the plan.

"The engines!"

Machado turned to see Gustavo. Damnit! Why didn't this kid listen?

Gustavo yelled out to make himself heard.

"We need to take out the engines!"

Machado whipped his sidearm out and started to pour his clip into the two engines. Bullet holes speckled the plastic shield but the boat kept surging forwards. The round of gunfire had startled the pirates into cover, but as Machado's clip emptied they trained their machine guns. Machado hit the deck, literally, as the firearms blossomed heat and noise. The carbon nano-weave rebuffed the projectiles and the swell ensured the pirates fired more wildly than Machado had. It only took one bullet though. He reloaded to try for the engine again but this time the pirates were ready. He was absolutely pinned down.

He could hear their boat bashing against the white caps and their engines thrumming up and down as the resistance of the water changed from peak to peak. If he could time it, he might be able to fire again when they would most thrown off. There was shouting and he looked over to see Gustavo clambering across the front of the boat with the fishing rod in hand.

"Gustavo! Stay down!"

He pulled himself up and fired at the pirates desperately trying to draw their fire. Meanwhile Gustavo cast the line out ahead of their boat. What was he doing? The reel suddenly burst into life spooling out a hundred metres of line in a matter of seconds before the entire rod was plucked from Gustavo's hands. The other sound that erupted was from the engines of the speed boat. First one, then both of the beasts screamed a high pitched whine. One buckled and they both went dead. In a heart-beat it was over. The pirates bobbed up and down like a rubber duck in the bath.

The silence rushed back as the pirates shrank into the distance.

"I'm sorry." said Gustavo, who appeared at his side.

Machado looked down at a pale and stricken face.

"For what?"

"I lost the fishing rod."

"What happened?"

"Well I figured that normal fishing line is a huge problem for boat engines. If the line was made of nano-wire…"

Machado stared back out at their would-be murderers and their newly entangled source of locomotion.

"Gustavo Delgato. You, are a god-damned legend."

Gustavo allowed himself a slight grin of relief.

"Now let's celebrate," said Machado "with some well-earned muesli bars and cordial."

Sewerage

Adam followed Chloe out of the air-conditioning and into the sun. His face contorted at the smell.

"Human waste doesn't smell like farts." she said.

Adam tried to speak but doing so required catching his breath and his body was trying to close up all entry points.

"It smells like shit." she continued, "You get used to it pretty quickly."

Adam took tiny gasps and tried to focus on keeping his breakfast inside. The sun was baking the top of the treatment pond and crispy turds sailed their way across the sludgy sea with every change of the wind. Chloe bounced along the steel bridge. It rattled and clanked. He moved to catch her but his progress was much more subdued.

"If you're going to puke," she called back over her shoulder, "best to do it in the primary pond rather than any of the others."

They put a distance between themselves and the 'swimming hole of despair'. Adam looked down and saw a thick black hose running the length of the path.

"Is this new?"

"Sure is. This entire section was an empty field until two weeks ago. We brought a combobulator in and got to work. It's incredible how quickly you can put in infrastructure when you don't have to transport materials. Have you used one?"

"We've got one at home that sits on the bench. My

girlfriend complains that it's taken the joy out of cooking."

"Bet she doesn't complain about the washing up though."

"What do you mean?"

"Well, dirty plates go in. Clean ones come out."

Adam stopped short. Chloe turned back to see his eyes wide and his jaw dropped.

"You've never thought to use it to clean stuff?" she said.

"I just… I mean you ask it for stuff. And you feed it the materials it needs. Where do the food scraps go?"

Chloe squinted her eyes and swallowed her comment. Adam was familiar with this scenario. Clever people. He despised them. Always patronising. Chuckling and shaking their heads in astonishment. Of course now that he thought about it, of course the scraps were just more materials for the device. But who has the energy to do all that thinking? It sapped his strength yet seemed to come so naturally to them. Like they enjoyed it. Adam's favourite thing to do was zone out. To just go blank. His girlfriend would ask him 'What are you thinking about?' then get defensive when he would inevitably reply 'nothing'. He wasn't hiding anything. There was nothing to hide. Sometimes he worried that perhaps there was some joy that was passing him by. He tried not the think about it. He succeeded.

They'd arrived at what looked a bit like a tall VW covered in black shade-cloth. Chloe began to explain.

"The waste comes in via the sewerage system and is pumped up into pretreatment. We filter out the trash and pump air into the solution to separate the solids from the fluids. Then primary pool, more aeration to separate the loose fluid from the sludge. The fluid goes to the secondary pool and the sludge goes to a dryer to be finished and to have its methane extracted. There are all sorts of options for the water at this point. Dozens of ways to process it depending on where in the environment you want to return it. You can even drink it if you pass it through a recycling plant. We don't do that here but some places pump the water straight back into the water supply."

Adam's breakfast made a jailbreak attempt but the guards were just fast enough to suppress it.

"So what part of the process," he asked through gritted teeth, "are you requesting authorisation to change?"

"The whole thing."

She pulled back the black cloth to show what looked a bit like a jet engine made out of painted black metal. He recognised the material. Everyone was becoming very familiar with the default graphene plate that 'the machine' preferred to dispense. Chloe pulled a large banana-yellow toggle switch and the machine started to hum.

"It takes in the wastewater straight from the primary pool. The sludge gets broken down into its components. Tada! Clean raw materials. We can even skip the pre-treatment stage if we want to but it's useful to be able to test for pathogens in the community. Also it's really interesting to see what some people flush."

She winked, but given the context Adam did not feel confident to extrapolate what this meant.

"How did you make it so big?" asked Adam. "I thought the biggest ones were only the size of a vending machine?"

"We asked a machine to make four quarters of a bigger machine and then we clipped them all together. Then we asked it to make this guy."

She slapped the side of the device and it let out a chiming 'ga-bong' sound.

She walked to the other side of the device with Adam in her wake.

"You'll see on this side the various solid materials get ejected."

Several transparent chutes dropped tiny dice into coloured

buckets.

"Each bucket is colour-coded. The pebbles are simple cubes. If you look at the base of the bucket you'll see that it's textured to catch them. They self arrange like honeycombs."

She grabbed a handful to show him. Adam involuntary jerked backwards.

"It's not poop anymore. These are the pure elements that were extracted. This is copper. That one's pure gold. And down this end the water gets flushed out."

Adam put his hands on the side of the pool and stared into the crystal clear depths. The engine continued to hum and a steady gushing of water slowly filled the large pool. Chloe walked up next to it.

"We can completely update the waste management and recover millions of dollars worth of raw materials. We just need you guys to double check our test results and sign off on the paperwork and we can start updating the entire complex."

Adam tried to digest the information.

"I can't believe it" he muttered.

"It's amazing isn't it? Only seconds ago this was faecal slop. And now…"

She cupped her hand under the output valve and sloshed the pure water on her face. Adam's insides flipped over and his breakfast finally made bail.

Gustavo was shocked awake by a bolt of lightning hitting close enough to feel. The feeble rays of pre-dawn streaked down the wall and he could see that Machado's berth was empty. After a month at sea he was becoming proficient in anticipating the bounce of the deck under him. It had been weeks since he'd been knocked on his arse so it was with a sense of bewilderment that after leaping from his bunk he found himself collecting his bruised form from the floor.

Thin bands of light flittered from low on the wall to high as the boat listed heavily from port to starboard. He grabbed at every surface that presented itself and cautiously made his way to the door. It opened onto a disaster zone. Detective Machado was gripping onto the guard rail as salt water sluiced across underfoot. Lightning cracked. Sails drummed as gusting wind lurched to and fro. Machado called out.

"GET INSIDE!"

His bellowed voice was all but carried away by the wind. A sudden squall of heavy rain pounded across the deck for a moment before easing to a downpour that steamed off Gustavo's brow. Again he was being treated like a child. Both of their lives were at stake and damnit, he was still the captain. He grabbed for one of the bright orange lifejackets that had become their day-to-day wear and zipped it up.

The trip around the Cape of Good Hope had been fraught but exciting. This was something else entirely. The boat's autopilot merrily crested one of the larger of the swells before skidding down into the churn again. For a brief moment the raindrops burst into yellow stars as they refracted the sunlight that streamed in from the horizon. A moment later they were obscured again. Gustavo's heart pounded as gravity shut off for a moment. The boom swung dangerously close to his head and he slid across the open deck.

"GUSTAVO!"

Gustavo looked towards Machado and saw he was yanking on a carabiner attached to his vest. He'd tied himself to the guard rail and Gustavo realised that this was exactly what he needed to do as well. The boat dug into the sea doubling his weight for a moment and drove a deluge in his direction. The flood pushed him across the deck and into the guardrail. He held on with all of the death grip that an eleven year old can muster and spluttered out the salt water that was trying to stow away inside his lungs.

Machado undid one of his clips and carefully climbed along the rail, before reattaching and unclipping the second. He looked like a very slow Spiderman. Finally he was close enough to talk.

"Gustavo! It's too dangerous out here. You've got to get back inside!"

"I'm not a kid! I'm the captain! It's my boat!"

Machado pressed his face in closely. Gustavo steeled himself against the macho intimidation that had come so many times before. Instead Machado wiped his thumb across Gustavo's forehead. He pulled it back and it was covered in blood. The dull throb he'd been ignoring began to stab at his temples.

"You're the captain!" said Machado. "That means it's my job to keep you safe so that you can get us where we're going."

Gustavo looked into his eyes, first in surprise and then in resolve.

"Now get inside, where it's safe!"

Gustavo nodded. He waited for a lull then dashed across the deck and into the cabin. Sunlight illuminated the raindrops again. Dazzling star bursts twinkled and a bright white tear opened in the sky to his left. Machado yelled. It wasn't a cloud. It was the crest of the biggest wave he'd ever seen. It pounded into the side of the boat. Carbon nanofibre strained and tore. Diamond windows exploded. Gustavo was turned upside-down. There was a terrible jolt and he found himself trying to breathe, swim and determine which way was up all at the same time.

The life jacket did its job and his tiny form spat from the surface in an eruption of bubbles. More waves bashed against him and he paddled urgently in circles trying to see anything other than churning suds. Finally he saw it. The vanishing white form of his boat as it sped autonomously away leaving him to bob insignificantly in the middle of the vast Indian Ocean.

The Garden of Artists

The BMW crested the hill and Julia's view out of the passenger side window switched from Spanish vineyard to architectural wonder.

"Wooow!" she gasped.

"Impressive, no?" said Luis, "This was all grazing land two months ago. Dry rocky dirt. Useless for agriculture. There are now over 100 families living here. The project is led by Pierre Rotriani. His firm was responsible for the Gatetown Pavilion in Madrid."

"Oh, I've been there. It's lovely but, it's nothing like this."

"The Gatetown Pavilion was the result of giving Mr Rotriani a budget of 140 million dollars. It won several awards. But this…"

The car slowed so they might fully appreciate the intricate masonry of the arched entry.

"This is what happens when he has no limitations but his own genius."

The dazzling sunlight of the Spanish winter vanished as the tidy german automobile crept through the arch. Beams of light criss-crossed the bonnet and molested the specks of dust in the air.

"All of this is crafted" said Luis. "The beams of light are always at the correct angle. Some sort of parabolic… thing, I think. The 'dust' is misted through to finish the effect."

They rolled into the light again and into a fantasy. Julia's jaw dropped. Intricate dynamic fountains were framed by the askew lines of the buildings. Enormous conical umbrellas provided shade and flashes of bold colour. Every shape had a match. Every colour had a compliment. It felt like a cross between the Guggenheim and a Dr. Suess book. Dozens of people lounged and conversed in the community spaces. Julia counted four bakeries and two chocolateries.

"This is… astounding" she managed.

"There are no limitations here. Every decision is to service Rotriani's grand vision."

They turned off the main roundabout and into a side street. Ornate pedestrian overpasses clasped from each facade across the roadway. Julia looked up at the sky and saw the entire area was encased in glass. The apartments rose three stories high and waterfalls cascaded between the balconies.

"We're entirely self-sufficient. This is traditionally a very dry area but we have machines that take the water out of the air and hydrate the city. The entire township has three layers of infrastructure. First is personal basements and parking. Second is waste water, plumbing, sewerage."

"And the third basement?"

Luis smiled.

"That's Rotriani's office."

Julia's attention snapped to the buttresses overhead. Sandstone joists slid from either side of the street and, with all the grace of an Olympic gymnast, formed a long solid ribbon above the street. Within moments a grey and white monorail passed silently overhead and the tracks quietly retreated again. Ahead of them a middle-aged gentleman with a beard re-adjusted his grip on the backpack and easel that hung over his shoulder. He scowled at the scooter-mounted children that squealed as they slalomed around him. Luis carefully guided the car past him and under another overpass. The clustered apartments separated to reveal a second bright square. It seemed like a theme park mountain. Stairs and walkways spiraled up around the summit that stood five or six stories in the air.

Luis pressed a button that had been inelegantly attached to his dashboard. A wedge of grass and pavement began to rise like a magician's assistant. Within moments it had revealed an empty parking space. Once they'd parked and made their way onto the grass the car started to descend again. Within moments the turf had hidden their vehicle away with nothing to signify what had happened but for a small lit pole that had slid itself out of the curb and was now making a charismatic chiming sound. Luis grabbed a ticket from the pole and it fell silent. He turned towards the gardens.

"This, Julia, is the Garden of Artists. In the spring these vines and plants will begin to cover the trellises. The aim is for this to be a great resource for painters and artists."

He gestured for her to follow him and he charged excitedly up the steps.

"There are one hundred and forty four of these platforms speckled about the structure. Each one has shelter, storage for equipment and mirrors for redirecting light."

He opened and closed umbrellas and cabinets as he illustrated his point. Julia looked around at the structure and the people she'd noticed enjoying the view she now realised were capturing it in oils and charcoal.

"We believe that in this new world where we are rapidly approaching post-scarcity that the most important people in the world will be the artists. Engineers and architects are creating amazing living spaces but in order to create something like this..."

He gestured broadly.

"... they will need to develop their sense of aesthetics. Under the careful eye of Pierre Rotriani our mission is to foster the great minds of our generation."

"I see."

"And this, Julia, is where you come in. You come very highly recommended. I was told that you can find anything, and you can do so, discretely."

"And what is it that the offices of Pierre Rotriani would like me to find?"

Luis' unflappable manner flapped for the first time. A deep concern fell over his face.

"Pierre Rotriani."

"He's missing?"

"He went on a sudden international trip. He said it was to Singapore but we believe that may not be the case. His last communication was that he'd return by the end of the week. That was three weeks ago."

"Well, perhaps I'd better take a look at his office."

"Do you think you can find him?"

She looked him in the eye and smiled a warm and reassuring smile.

"I'll show you how I do *my* art."

Binoculars

Machado watched the hull of the boat stay steady and the world revolved a quarter turn around it. The sail sandwiched between the crashing wave and the sea surface. A bolt of pain started at his hip and then cascaded through ever joint. The clasp that connected him to the boat had yanked him down into the sea. The pressure of water and a flood of bubbles. The ballast pulled the vessel upright again and he was in morning sunlight. The canopy of the boat was missing from its usual silhouette. It flailed off the starboard side of the vessel like a playful labrador yanking and janking the usually clean pathway of their progress. The main sail had been damaged and, untethered, flickered like a candle flame. These materials were strong but the rogue wave had been stronger.

Gustavo… wasn't… there.

The cool salt water wicked under Machado's raincoat and into his inner clothes. His fingers twitched towards an undo key that wasn't there. His mind battled trying to both awaken from this nightmare and find a solution to a problem he knew he couldn't solve.

The boat moved forwards.

He slipped and skidded across the deck and grabbed at the wheel. It span impotently. The data screen mocked him with 'Authorisation Required'. He jabbed at the screen. 'Authorisation Required'. Wiping his eyes with the sleeve of his bright yellow rain jacket effectively delivered more salt water to his face.

The boat moved forwards.

He locked his arm into a support beam to steady himself and then scanned the horizon for the orange dot of life-jacket nestled amongst the churn and the small scared Portuguese boy, himself nestled inside of that dot. There! He yanked open the outer storage hatch and pulled the binoculars to his face whilst simultaneously repressing the horror that there was nothing he could do to the stop the boat. Despite the damage it happily kept its course, like a spaceship drifting from an abandoned astronaut. Machado trained the lenses on Gustavo. The boy appeared for a moment between waves. He wasn't yelling. He wasn't scrambling. He reached for the sky, his pinky outstretched yearning to get as much height as he could. Like everything Gustavo did, it was thoughtful and calculated. This incredible child was being sucked into the void. Each wave revealing him to be smaller and smaller again until finally he couldn't be found. Lost at sea. Gone.

The boat moved forwards.

Salt water continued to run down Machado's face. He lowered the binoculars and tried to regulate his breathing. The sail had come loose, perhaps he could pull it down and somehow guide the boat around? Glancing at the semi-submerged canopy he knew this wouldn't work. The boat was smart enough to compensate. His knees shook and he collapsed into his seat. He had to do... something. But of course he'd been trying to turn this boat around for months now. It was impossible. Gustavo would still have his hand out waiting to be rescued but he too knew it was impossible. Smart kid probably knew he was doomed the moment he hit the water. The boat would leave him and could never come back.

Waiting to be rescued. Knew it was impossible.

...

If he knew it was impossible… why was he waving for rescue? He bobbed up and down in his own brain as the boat did the same in the swell. The pinky finger isn't the longest finger. He looked down at his own hands and made the same shape that Gustavo had. Was it a message? A code? He turned his hand over to look at the knuckles, the fingernail, then flipped it back over. The bright morning sunlight rippled across his wet fingerprints.

click

He pressed his pinky finger to the navigation screen and it blinked green. 'Login Successful'. For an infinitesimal moment Machado considered letting the boy drown. He tapped the Autopilot button and the boat came under his control. Yanking the wheel around provided resistance and the length of the vessel slowly span in the brine. Messages streamed down the screen, 2 months of diagnostic updates. The most recent ones appearing all in uppercase. The compass stated a westerly course and Machado straightened her up. There was a lot of data on the screen he didn't understand, but he could at least see his GPS course. All he needed to do was follow that in reverse.

He wasn't travelling fast but for the first time in months he was finally travelling in the right direction.

Mirage

Craig Palin wanted people to see him as a rugged individualist. He had recently dedicated his life to succeeding at each one of the things that other individualists did. He was yet to realise the irony. Truth be told he was yet to realise a lot of things. His expensive racing boat sliced though the water like a duck through a money-bin. Jason liked metaphors that celebrated wealth. The hull dashed at the chop and he let the sea spray splatter his face. A movie hero on an adventure.

He hated every moment of it. He longed for the comfort of the posh retreats of his twenties. The mani-pedies. The keratin smoothing. The vapid instagram girls who orbited him in the hope that his wealth made him more interesting. But he wasn't interesting. He was dull. Dull and loud. It had taken him a decade and a half of his adulthood but he'd finally developed enough self-awareness to see that at least. Being dull isn't a problem if you're quiet. Plenty of his more "mysterious" friends were happy to continue that ruse. But he loved being loud. He'd happily listen to the sound of his own voice for hours. Or at least, that's what he thought.

He'd recorded a dozen episodes of a podcast before it had even occurred to him to listen back to one. It had moved him to tears. So utterly devoid of content. So vacuous. Self-indulgent tripe. The rare iTunes reviews had been right. It was hard to write them off as jealous trolls when they'd hit the nail so accurately on the proverbial head.

And so he'd thrown a party. A big celebration to announce

his trip around the world. The shopping had been the best part. Oh the shopping. The various types of boats. The list of high tech materials. The trendy unnecessary gadgets. And of course he finally had something to talk about.

"Yes he was going all the way around the world."

"No he'd never sailed before."

"Yes he was a bit scared but mostly he was excited."

He finally felt like someone. The sensation of being welcomed into the conversation that had eluded him since he was a child. That episode of the podcast had resulted in something "actually listenable".

The actual process was bloody horrible. Staring at the water. Barely any Internet. Eating that horrible long lasting food. What he wouldn't give for a seat at 'Exhalations' and their degustation menu right now. He almost felt like crying. Perhaps he could just stop at one of the Pacific islands and hide out there. Fly home in five months to great acclaim. It might raise questions if he didn't turn up with the boat he supposed. He resigned himself to this useless pilgrimage.

A thick cloud passed across both his heart and the rest of his organs. He looked up at the lack of sunshine and saw the sky had darkened above him and outwards to the south. 'Great!' he thought. More bloody rain. On his right (He hadn't learned the nautical term) was a great glowing castle. Probably a kilometre or two to the south. The rain had just started behind it. Grey curtains of precipitation obscured the skyline except where the castle stood. Like a giant cardboard cut-out beaming out a sky blue. He instinctively grabbed at his phone when the enormous beaming walls flickered like an airport departure sign. They vanished. Just squalls of rain remained. He took a photo of the rain clouds anyway.

'This' he thought to himself, 'could be a whole episode'.

Recovery

The GPS showed a ball of wool with the route scribbling back and forth through the sea. The going was slow. The canopy hung upside-down off the port side and the tiny electric engine was struggling to compensate against the constant push of seawater. Its tiny electric brain tried going forwards and would list to the right, then it would try to turn left until it was lined up with its waypoint, then it would try to go forward and list to the right. Machado turned off the way-finding and had been manually zig-zagging the waves for hours now. The rising sun vanished behind the cloud cover.

Despite his barely suppressed terror that he wouldn't be able to find Gustavo, it did feel good to be in charge again. To be at the whims of a machine that was at the whims of a child… it had been sapping at his sense of autonomy. To get his hands around the ship's wheel and have it resist and then yield to his touch… it felt real. The chop splashed against the submerged canopy. He had tried to yank it aboard but it had rather effectively cupped several tonnes of the ocean. There was a tiny bilge pump he could set to work on the problem but he suspected it would be a lot easier to repair if he wasn't… he paused to gather his anxieties and frustrations of the day…

"IN THE MIDDLE OF THE GODDAMNED OCEAN!"

The breeze whipped away his angry statement and the air was again silent but for the lapping of the sea, the creak of the rigging, and the barely audible trilling of a plastic whistle. He

113

blinked back the salt from his eyes and clocked himself on the cheek rushing the binoculars to his face. A blink of light caught his attention. There! In the distance, was a big white seagull sitting on top of very upset young man. Machado reefed the boat to the west. He then cursed at the canopy and pulled the wheel slightly in the opposite direction.

The electric motors hummed its song as the distance between them closed. A startled gull leapt off Gustavo's head in fright, wheeled around calling out bird curse words before alighting on the stern. Machado cut the engine and the vessel span around its accidental sea anchor. The port side gracefully came up to meet Gustavo. A boat hook was proffered and he was unceremoniously dragged to the back of the boat where Machado grabbed the back of the life jacket and heaved him backwards where his weight overcame him and Gustavo crashed on top of him and into his arms. For a moment he hugged the child in relief but then his police training kicked in. He let go and started checking the boy for injuries.

"Are you hurt? Are you injured at all?"

Gustavo didn't respond.

"Gustavo?"

The boy failed to meet his eyes and stared mutely over his shoulder.

"Hey! You okay?"

Finally the boy's bright brown eyes met his own and a feeble voice whispered…

"no"

…before staring again over his shoulder. Machado looked behind him and the mournful call of the gull met him.

"He pooped in my hair."

Machado looked at Gustavo's head, then at his hand where he'd been checking him for injuries. It was caked with sticky white muck. The lack of sleep, the anxiety, the relief, and the poop finally crashed up against his resolve. His strong shoulders shuddered and his face burst into a brash, and somewhat manic, laughter.

The boy's eyes went wide with the shock of the noise. Machado showed his palms smeared as they were. Gustavos face burst into a grin and he was laughing too. They'd had a very emotional morning and there were bigger problems to face but for the moment they could just enjoy the sound of each other's hooting laughter.

The sun peeked out from the clouds. Machado rinsed his hands in the sea and enjoyed the absence of forward movement. This amazing vessel was quiet in operation but two months of constant churning towards the destination was grating. To have a moment of calm was a relief.

"It's my fault" he heard Gustavo mutter.

The canopy of the boat lolled in the water to the port side and Gustavo was mourning its lack of integrity.

"When I designed it, the boat needed to inflate to full size. The bulk of the components are woven graphene but along this line they needed to clip in. I don't know enough about engineering to... I shouldn't have..."

His voice started to catch. He'd shown himself to be competent and even heroic in an emergency. Machado watched him trying to hide his tears. He put his large calloused hand on the boy's shoulder.

"We're all doing the best we can Gus. We'll fix it. Between you, me and the seagull, we've got the brains to solve this problem."

Gustavo took a big breath, trying to will his tears back into his face and said almost to himself, "There's no... such thing as a seagull. Gulls live on the land and only come to the sea to hunt."

"Then what's he doing out here in the middle of the..."

The gull had become more skittish as attention focused on

it and after a moment awkwardly leaped into the sky and
took off towards the north.

"FOLLOW THAT BIRD!"

Collective

General Abrams stared out the windows at the manicured landscaping. The White House was just out of view but the lawns and statues he could see still filled him with a gentle reassurance.

"So tell me Tanner. I don't understand why some shit-hole countries banding together is freaking you out. It seems like tin-pot nonsense again."

"You've heard of the Combobulator, sir?"

Abrams' hand twitched and he suppressed the desire to comb his bold white moustache with his finger tips. The damnable therapist his wife had dragged him along to had described this as a "self-soothing behaviour". Self soothing? Was he a toddler?! From that day forward he vowed to remain completely unsoothed. Some would describe this as a state of high anxiety. So be it. It made sense to him that the man with his finger so close the nation's weapons should be on a hair trigger. It made you alert, and ready.

"This is the god-damned genie machine I've been hearing about. Yes, I've heard of it. Disrupting trade throughout Europe. My 401K is a mess."

"Chad received one and it propagated rapidly. It's put an enormous amount of power in the hands of the workers."

"I'll bet. Free booze and TVs. I can't imagine there's anyone there who wants to do an honest day's work."

"That's one of many surprises sir. Once the people weren't working for survival a union of sorts formed to share this tech with as many people as possible."

Tanner opened his dossier and spread a handful of photos across the desk. Both men leaned over them. Abrams refused to have chairs in his office. Felt it made a man too relaxed. The photos showed people who would fit into this category perfectly. Shining happy faces hanging off the side of rickety old trucks packed to the gills with Combobulators. Modular housing replacing old tin shacks. Children raising up diamond glasses filled with fresh clean water or toasting with bottles of what purported itself to be 'Cork-a-cola'.

"I can't imagine the warlords are taking this well."

"They've lost a lot of their cachet sir. There was an uptick in violence to begin with, but their militias were mostly ranked with people doing a dangerous job just to get the things they needed to survive. Now that those needs have been met they're more hesitant to put themselves in harm's way. There was some violence on the borders because, as you know, the machine won't work after they cross into another country. Raiding marauders would flood across to strip the villagers of their new-found wealth."

He pulled another glossy photograph from his folder.

"Judas?"

The imagine showed a dark grey truck-trailer with the word 'Judas' stencilled on the side. Behind it lay dozens more.

"They call them Judas-boxes. They're filled with all the niceties that the machines can provide. Rather than attacking the villagers, the marauders can come in, hook up the trailers and tear off into the night. No shots fired."

"Who organises these? How do they pay them?"

"Volunteer collectives sir. Turns out when people don't have to work for a living they work for a better life."

Abrams brow furrowed. 'Bullshit' he thought. If everything he knew about those people was true (it wasn't) then there's no way that could be true (it was).

"So where does it all fall down?" he said with utmost confidence.

"Well, it was working okay sir, but once Spain capitulated to Portugal, well, that's when the protests began."

"The people of Chad wanted to invade? Makes sense. That's what happens when anyone gets a taste of the good life. They just want more."

"No sir, the surrounding countries wanted to become part of what they're now calling 'Africania'. Niger, Cameroon, Benin. City-wide protests and in some case riots. There were even protests in Chad that the government needed to offer assistance.

"Protesting to offer assistance?"

These are people who have struggled everyday. They now find themselves with more than they could have ever hoped for. All they want to do is share it."

He pulled out a map of the dark continent, bright with addendums and notes.

"What's this?"

Abrams pointed to the very west coast.

"Gambia sir. Or at least, what was once called Gambia. They're the most recent member of this union. They're another part of Chad."

"The same country scattered all over the map. Is there any precedence for this?"

"Well it seems to be functioning as a commonwealth of sorts. Combobulator tech is being shared to each country. The poor are being fed, the middle class are getting big screen TVs. Somalia and Tanzania are both days away from joining. It's all happening very quickly."

Abrams was leaning on the table. He moved his left hand to cover his right hand which was in urgent danger of drumming out a tattoo of self-soothing beats.

"So what are the ramifications of this?"

"Our biggest problem is resources. When the population are satiated there's no way to motivate them to operate the mines. Many of the world's largest natural deposits are in that area. With a population desperate for basic necessities there's never been a problem keeping them manned but now many are working at 20% capacity. The mines there are incredibly dangerous and now there just isn't an incentive. On top of that they no longer need to sell the resources for a pittance. The machines will run with the raw materials. It's become a seller's market."

Abrams turned to the window again to stare at the people walking their pure-bred pets. Jogging in designer sportswear. Driving their European cars. All of this was at risk because a bunch of foreigners figured they were too good to work.

"Deadbeats!" he cursed under his breath without even the merest hint of self-awareness.

Île Saint-Paul

Gustavo used his front teeth to plane a sliver of energy bar chocolate into his mouth. He allowed it to rub all around the inside of his cheeks, coating every surface with a thin sugary film. He swallowed. A rush of delight after hours cold and hungry in the water. They had worked out that their rations would limit them to less than a bar each per day. With that in mind Gustavo had become a zen master of eeking out every droplet of joy that each bar had to give. After a quarter of the bar had been completed he carefully folded the wrapper into a very clever origami seam that he had seen on the Internet. It had purported to seal any half finished product shut again and so it was with a sense of mild frustration that Gustavo watched it immediately start to unfurl. He jammed it against the edge of the cabinet in the now sun-drenched kitchen.

"There's another one" Machado called out enthusiastically.

Gustavo turned to look in the direction he was pointing and saw yet another gull wheeling its way through the sky.

"They've got to be nesting somewhere close."

He stroked at his now plush beard before continuing "How far can gulls fly in a day?"

The grizzled policeman now looked more like a grizzled bear for the thick beard that was settling on his face. Gustavo absent-mindedly stroked his own chin then looked into the mirror in the bathroom at his much less impressive growth. Not a follicle. There was however a nasty bruise blossoming across his temple when some unknown part of the vehicle had kissed him with little warning and even less consent. He touched it gently expecting it to hurt. As expected, it hurt.

The early afternoon sun had warmed up and dried the deck of the boat and was now content baking the pair. Gustavo smeared some more sunscreen on his face and ears before offering a blob to his second in command. Machado looked a lot more like a pirate these days. Thick beard, leathery skin, torn clothing. As the trip was initially conceived for one person there was nothing in the wardrobe that remotely fit the detective. As uncomfortable as Gustavo was, he at least had clean dry underpants to change into.

"Three birds. There. No wait! FOUR!"

Machado seemed to be having such a good time hunting for birds Gustavo didn't want to tell him about the island that had appeared almost directly ahead of them. He stayed silent wondering how many birds Machado would count before seeing what was directly in front of him. It turned out that number was eleven.

"Gustavo! Land!" Machado called out doing little in the way of quashing his pirate appearance.

"Machado! You did it!" Gustavo replied.

A beaming smile broke the shaggy face and the "Dread Pirate Machado" yanked the wheel to the port to ensure their path remained as straight as possible despite a good chunk of semi-submerged canopy doing its best to draw them into tight circles. If he'd seen through Gustavo's ruse he hadn't let on, or maybe he didn't care.

It was mid-afternoon when they got close enough to see the pounding surf dashing against the vertical cliff face. Hundreds of gulls swarmed the crenelations of the rock surface. Their calls felt somehow mocking. The boat's electric engine whined its single note melody along to the percussion of the water slamming against the unscalable wall.

Twenty minutes later they were skirting the south side of

the island and the wall was lower but no less impregnable. There didn't seem to be much foliage. Grass. Birds. Taller grass.

"We can't eat grass. But we can eat birds." Machado replied when Gustavo shared his observation.

"More importantly" he continued, "We'll be able to fix the canopy… If we can just find a damned place to land!"

Like a cloud lifting to reveal the sunlight after a week of rain, the east side of the island hove into view. The cliffs on both sides slid down to the sea. With the westerly winds occluded the surf was calm and inviting. As they crept closer they saw an inlet to a huge bay. The electric motor kept humming as they crawled between the two sand banks flanking the entrance. Gustavo looked into the crystal clear waters and saw fish flickering by. Machado pointed out a shark and Gustavo though that was pretty cool. When he lifted his head he saw steep but climbable slopes of grass with nests dotted about the surface. It seemed that they were in the centre of an enormous crater.

"Look, there!" he called out.

They both focused their attention on a collection of buildings on the north bank of the bay. Machado pulled the wheel to starboard (or more accurately he stopped pulling quite so hard to port) and the boat arced around to run up against the edge of the bay.

They wobbled up the rocky shoreline feeling solid ground for the first time in well over a month. The structures turned out to be less exciting than they'd hoped. Stone walls with ceilings that had long since dropped to the floor and decayed. Gustavo wandered closer to the beach and here he found a large pine box. Weathered but maintained. Machado joined him as he opened it and inside were ropes, a bottle of water, a Swiss army knife, and a collection of rations.

"Jackpot!" said Machado as he yoinked them from the box.

"There's writing here. It says it's the official emergency box of Île Saint-Paul. It's French."

"Island of Saint-Paul? Big fan of the Beatles?"

Gustavo had no idea what Machado was talking about but he seemed pleased with himself. They returned to the boat and bailed water from the upturned canopy. Now they had a bracing position and it wasn't constantly refilling itself they were able to hoist the whole thing back into position. The sun set and they shared a single ration meal. Even Gustavo was surprised at how eager he was to consume the vegetable half-block in the tray.

With real food in their stomachs and a roof over their heads they both passed into a deep and deserved slumber. The gull calls quietened and the waxing moon vanished over the horizon. In the pitch dark the clock quietly struck midnight and a small logo that looked like a compass silently illuminated.

Three Types of Portuguese

The Parisians believe themselves to be the true French. Everyone else in France knows that this is not the case. Daniel LaCroix strode through the Tuileries Garden eyeing the crowds of people that had formed around the recently installed Combobulator. He corrected himself. Recently congealed Combobulator.

Daniel had grown up in a small town along the coast of Brittany. While he had been living and working in Paris for over a decade now, in his heart he felt that he was 'true French'. Now the French government had conceded to the public's wishes and become a state of Portugal. 'Thousands of years of fighting and then we just handed it all over for magic vending machines.'

He checked his watch and slowed his pace to a stop. With a little time on his side he decided to watch the 'theatre of greed' play out. He pulled out his cigarette pack and selected a crumpled white shaft of tobacco. The lid of the pack snapped shut and somewhere in his brain a Pavlovian message activated. Anticipation. Serotonin. In one fluid motion the cigarette slipped between his lips and his lighter snapped a tiny explosion into being. The flame was protected from the wind but the cigarette failed to light. Daniel slid his cigarette back into the pack and tucked it away. It had been four years since he'd inhaled that rich tobacco cloud but he still couldn't shake the habit. He'd dipped his pack into flame proof liquid and now he could practice the customs without the carcinogens.

The cluster of people around the machine seemed eager but not aggressive. In Britain they'd be lining up in queues. Daniel took a sense of national pride that his fellow countrymen continued to rebel against authority even in this simple task. It had always struck him as strange that the Parisians considered themselves the true French. It seemed so arrogant, which he reflected, was definitely 'on brand'. It didn't matter then, what the rest of the country thought. The idea of a Frenchman was in their minds. Now the whole country was Portuguese. But at the same time it was French. There were the Parisian French, who were now Portuguese. There were the Portuguese, (This included the Spanish) and then there were all the cities and towns in the rest of France. They were Portuguese now too. Daniel turned this idea over in his head. 'That didn't stop us from being the *true French* though' he mulled to himself.

He checked his watch and decided there was still plenty of time for another cigarette.

Full Larder

The machine door clicked and revealed a plate of steaming spaghetti bolognaise. The sauce slid down through the perfectly cooked threads of pasta. Tiny fractals of parmesan cheese adorned it like a bride's veil. A glistening fork stuck out of the meal. An arrow in a successful hunt. Proper food. Machado could almost hear Gustavo salivating.

To escape the hot morning sun they sat in the ship's cosy kitchenette. Machado had a full steak dinner with mashed potatoes. A bowl of buttered broccoli sat steaming on the table.

"Eat slowly! We've both been eating very frugally. If you rush your first real meal in a month you'll make yourself sick."

Gustavo silently met Machado's gaze and his second forkful slowed to bullet-time on route to his mouth. There was already sauce on his chin. The seasoned detective chuckled and cut himself his own mouthful. His first bite was easily in the top five moments of his life. His second was still in the top twenty. After weeks of sugary treats, his cravings, not just his appetite were being satiated. The emergency rations they'd recovered from the island had a well expired 'best by' date though Machado suspected they'd never been what could be considered 'best'.

Where-as this steak… it was the first time he'd tried 'gastrome de machiné' and his concerns that it would be sub-par were unfounded. There was something missing though.

127

He jumped up to the machine and asked for a pint of beer. The machine clicked and he took out a small glass of beer. A half-pint. His brow furrowed as he read the bright warning label on the glass.

'Alcohol consumption can lead to health issues. Research suggests more than one standard drink a day is doing you damage.'

Machado scoffed. This from the same machine that had recommended he try MDMA. He returned to his meal. They ate in contented silence for a few minutes before Gustavo spoke up.

"I wonder why it activated again. Does the machine think we're back in Portugal"

"C'est français" said Machado grabbing the empty army rations pack and indicating the language. "Maybe France is part of the machine's list of allowed countries now. Whatever the reason it looks like we're back in business."

"I wonder how it knows." said Gustavo between single coiled threads of spaghetti.

"Satellites I suppose. It's all satellites these days."

"But it would have to be a secret. Hidden codes in the data."

Machado's fork tapped in the air like a fairy Godmother's wand making a salient point.

"Your little mind never turns off does it? Always trying to work things out."

Gustavo shrugged.

"It's just fun to think about things, you know?"

At which point he did just that. Machado watched him carefully. His lips would occasionally jiggle like the words in his head were overflowing out onto his pasta. His eye would dart from side to side looking at the forms in his mind's eye.

"Do policemen have a secret code?"

"Huh?"

"Like if you're in a shoot-out and you need to tell someone to go around the back."

Machado smirked.

"No, nothing like that. A number of my coworkers can barely understand plain Portuguese. I doubt they have the mental fortitude to deal with secret codes."

"Oh"

Gustavo's brow furrowed.

"Actually, there used to be. There were "ten" codes. I think we tried to use them in the seventies but it lead to too many misunderstandings so we just use plain language now."

"Oh, like 10-4?"

"Yes. There're a whole list but officers would get mixed up. 10-1 meant bad reception. 10-12 meant stay where you are. 10-32 meant person with gun. And let me assure you, you didn't want to mix those up."

"Maybe they should have used easier things to remember. Like fruit."

Machado grinned.

"Pineapple! Pineapple! Stay where you are!"

Gustavo spluttered sauce all over the table as Machado continued.

"Suspect with banana! Do not approach until Apple!"

Gustavo howled with laughter and Machado felt a warmth he'd not felt in a long time. He wasn't silly often. It felt good.

"What we need is a code that means 'Don't fall out of the boat'"

Gustavo was suddenly dead serious and Machado wondered if he'd accidentally stepped onto some particularly thin egg shells.

"I think I can create reinforcing to attach the canopy properly this time."

"Any suggestion that prevents us being washed overboard I support. If you hadn't been wearing that life jacket... I'd never have spotted you."

Gustavo's hand went to the torch in his pocket. He'd taken to carrying it with him at all times. A little talisman to protect him from the sea.

Machado continued, "We should probably create some more fishing equipment and fill the larders with…"

He jammed a fork into a steaming bud of broccoli to emphasise his point.

"…vegetables."

Gustavo looked in dismay at the plate of greens. He picked out the smallest bud and reluctantly put it in his mouth. After a moment of chewing…

"Iz pretty good… for broccoli."

He added more to his plate.

"It's almost like your body is trying to stave off scurvy." said Machado grinning.

"At any rate" he continued, "we can stock the boat with food, drink… clothing!"

His eyes lit up.

"Underpants"

Gustavo burst into another fit of laughter. Machado beamed.

"We can finally go home"

Gustavo's face fell.

"But what about Handout Miracle Algorithm?"

Machado took a sip of his tiny beer.

"Gustavo. We've already escaped death multiple times. We can't go adventuring around the globe."

"But who made the Combobulator? Don't you want to know who's responsible?"

Machado stroked his beard.

"Whoever did this, they've completely turned Porto upside-down. I don't even know what sort of life we're returning to. If everyone has access to whatever they want, why would anyone ever work again? The person who did this, they have a bigger plan. But it's way beyond my pay grade. I was just trying to stop a drug dealing vending machine."

He looked Gustavo in the eyes.

"And to keep some poor kid from ending up on the streets. It's time for this to end. We're going home."

Tears welled in Gustavo's eyes.

"I don't have one." he whispered.

Machado had months now of studying the boy. He was a master manipulator. If Machado dropped him into foster care he knew that wouldn't be the end of it, but what could he do? He closed his eyes for a moment. He just wanted to go home.

"Gustavo. I consider you a friend now. When we return to Portugal you'll always have me on your side. We can find a foster home where you fit, and I'll be able to help you whenever you need."

"I'll run away."

"I'll find you."

"I'll make another boat. I'll try again."

"AND BE ATTACKED BY PIRATES AGAIN?! AND GET KNOCKED OVERBOARD AGAIN?! AND FOR WHAT?!"

Gustavo's eyes were wide. The plates had rattled and the beer was spilled. Machado's voice went quiet making the anger even more unsettling.

"We don't even know who's at the end of this invitation. It could be drug lords, or pedophiles. It could be a god-damned super villain for all we know."

Gustavo opened his palms and plastered his face with a reassuring smile.

Machado snarled, "Don't do that! I know what you're doing and it's patronising."

Gustavo whipped his hands to his side and lowered his gaze.

"m S'rry"

Machado stared at the spilled beer and the trembling boy and sighed.

He grabbed the crockery and pushed them into the machine. Its compass rose glowed bright for a moment as it disassembled the molecules. Machado marched into the washroom and jerked the door shut. A moment later he reappeared.

"Underpants!" he snapped at the machine.

A Shave Too Tight

Glenn Ceaser puffed his cheeks and gazed out of his office window at the London Skyline. When he was a boy it had seemed the view was respectable. Historic. Now it looked like a child's crib. Shiny bulbous objects. Giant spinning disks. He wondered if prior generations had had the same reaction to the Tower Bridge, St Pauls Cathedral, Big Ben. For a moment he imagined a filthy 17th century merchant looking up at the splendour of the recently completed wonder of engineering and remarking to himself 'Bit bloody ornate'.

Behind him, waiting patiently, was one of the company's tech boffins. He always felt it valuable to keep them waiting. Their world was all computers and all they wanted to do was rush. Glenn remembered the days when you'd send your mail out and that was the end of it. Off to lunch and down the club in time for tee-off. Now you had responses to your first mail before the last one had been sent. Rush Rush Rush. Work Work Work. It was important that everyone was encouraged to take time.

On his office wall was a mock up poster he'd commissioned himself. In it an ornately carved frame around a mirror. The reflection was a man in a towel, his cheeks covered in lather. He stood like a soldier, ready to shave, his weapon at hand. Eyes closed in silent meditation. The anticipation of a cathartic practice. In big bold arial font... Take the time to enjoy a Ceaser Blade™.

The marketing team had hated it, of course. Who was he to

be offering ideas to sell their razors. He was only the boss. They ended up going with something involving helicopters.

He turned to finally engage with the boffin.

"So, Eric, what do you have for me?"

"Nigel, sir"

"Of course, Nigel."

"You've been following what's been happening in Portugal sir? The Combobulators."

"I've heard of them, yes."

It had been hard not to. Every second article in his economy magazines were about them. He could never tell at a glance if he was looking at market trends or an earthquake readout. He supposed, in some way, it was both.

"We got a sample of razors created by the machine and we've been doing tests."

He whipped out some stiff cardboard backed illustrations. The boy had come prepared. Glenn appreciated the theatre.

"This is a close up photograph of our best blade. Tempered stainless steel. Twelve percent chromium. Next to it, the machine's blade."

"They look identical." said Glenn with a sense of pride and relief.

Nigel pulled a second card out. On the left it appeared to be a black and white photo of the Alps with all the creases and crenelations of several hundred thousand years of erosion. On the right, the machine's blade remained sharp and effective.

"This is after four shaves, sir. Their blade doesn't deteriorate."

Glenn drummed his fingers on his desk.

"How do they do it?"

"It's not steel, it's graphene."

He pulled out a third card.

"We put them both under an electron microscope. In our

blades you can seem the shape of the iron crystals where they've cooled into position."

Glenn had once holidayed in Ireland. He and his girlfriend at the time had marvelled at the Giant's Causeway. Thousands of naturally formed hexagonal pillars made from the cooling of basalt. The stainless steel under an electron microscope reminded him of this. Like a chaotic honeycomb created by demented bees.

"It's this chaos that allows for the edge of the blade to erode away under both physical pressures and chemical ones."

"Chemical?"

"Oxidisation."

He pulled out a forth card.

"This is the machine's blade."

Glenn's eyes didn't really know what to do. It looked like it was moving.

"It's an optical illusion, sir."

Glenn's attention slide around the image like it was trying to hold a bar of soap. It seemed like an illustration of children's race cars all snapped together vying for first place but never changing position.

"Because every molecule has been carefully placed there are no imperfections. No fault lines. The atoms in the blades may break down atomically but structurally they'll keep their shape for months of use. Maybe years."

"Okay… Okay, so how do we make these? If we can replicate this we can sell them as… long term investment blades. Premium blades."

"We can't sir. This technology, it's completely new. And it's going to destroy us."

"That seems a bit portentous. Surely this is just a material science problem."

"We've been forging steel for thousands of years. The last

four hundred years have honed that process. The last twenty years have milked what little blood there is from these ores. The gains we're making now are incremental. This is nothing like that."

He looked at the photograph again.

"I've never seen anything like this before. No-one has. You may as well ask me to build you a flying saucer."

Glenn Ceaser looked from card to card.

"Alright… is that all?"

"Yes, sir."

"Leave these with me."

Nigel handed over the illustrations and left the office.

"Thank you Eric" said Glenn absent-mindedly.

He'd run this company since taking over from his father. He'd battled the super-corporations and the consumer advocacy groups and won every time. He'd find a solution. He always had. He tried to stand up but his legs were trembling.

The first of many earthquakes.

The Fastest Route

Gustavo toyed with the boat's computer. There had to be a back door. If he could just lock Machado out again. The predawn sky was brightening.

'Authorisation Required'

He studied the device searching for a reset button. He hadn't designed that in. It was just naive optimism at this point. Dumb. He should have planned for this. His brain berated him. It didn't matter that his situation was so far 'off book' there was no way he could have predicted it. His brain hated him anyway. Dumb dumb dumb.

'Authorisation Required'

"I'm making myself a coffee" bellowed Machado popping his head into view from the cabin.

Gustavo leapt and his blood went cold. Machado laughed a belly laugh and wandered back inside the cabin. Shame rushed through Gustavo's veins and lodged deep in his brain where, in twenty years time it could pop back out while his adult self tried to sleep. Another failure.

Machado returned to berate him. He was holding a steaming cup of coffee and a hot chocolate.

"Here you go kid."

Gustavo considered refusing it out of spite but he was already taking his first sip by the time he'd gathered his thoughts.

"Sorry for startling you. It was just too tempting."

What was this? A trick?

"Why aren't you… angry?"

"Because I knew that as soon as it was possible you'd try to hijack us again. You can be a real… You're driven."

He grinned into his coffee.

"I don't blame you. When I was your age I wanted to take off by myself too. Create my own destiny."

"And is this the time you give me a rousing speech about how important it is to rely on the advice of adults?"

"Shit no! I love working by myself."

Gustavo snorted hot chocolate all down his shirt.

"Look, I know you're angry and you want to solve this mystery. I'd love to know too, but I've got a duty of care."

"I can take care of myself."

"You're going to believe that for many years before it's true."

He stared up at the crater that surrounded him before adding, "I know I still do."

"Duty of care? You're not my Grandpa. You're not even my foster family. Who even are you that you care at all? You're just some nosey cop."

A storm cloud rumbled over Machado's face.

"The fact of the matter is that you're just a kid and now I'm the captain. We may have food and repairs but we're still in the middle of the god-damned ocean. I'm not just trying to keep you safe. I'm trying to keep me safe too. You make this big song and dance about being brave but it's easy to be brave when you don't appreciate the danger at hand."

Gustavo imagined that he could see anger flashing around Machado like koi in a pond but the grizzled cop continued to keep a level voice.

"I'm going to do what's best for us but I'd like you to be involved in the decision. We could sail back the way we came but we'd be sailing into head winds until we reached Cape Hope. I suggest we sail east to Perth. There we can sell the boat to buy plane tickets back to Portugal."

"But it's my boat!"

"You got it for free out of a vending machine. I think we can get you another one." said Machado dismissively.

"Fine" said Gustavo.

So much time wasted. Handout Miracle Algorithm. He didn't know what this invitation was for, but he hated the idea that it was time sensitive. At least they were heading east. That was still the right direction. They sat drinking their beverages as the predawn became post-predawn.

Machado finished the last mouthful of his first and last "proper coffee" for many months then said, "I'm not just a nosey cop, Gustavo. I'm a nosey friend."

He winked and then stood up to start preparing for the trip.

Gustavo stared into the bottom of his glass at the blob of cocoa powder that resolutely refused to detach as per section 14.7 of the universe's rulebook.

'Friend?' whispered Gustavo under his breath.

Machado was getting as good at lying as he was.

Visible Prey

Captain Ian Thompson uttered a very manly noise and kicked at his wastepaper bin. It skittered away under his desk where it would remain until some underling would come in to replace all the broken and bent items. He felt like Moby Dick chasing his own white whale. (Captain Thompson was not well read.) He stared out the porthole at the horizon rolling to and fro and pondered the article that had inspired his anti-receptacle attitude.

The left wing newspapers, what few remained, were always complaining that 'Sovereign Borders' was a waste of money. Now this sentiment was bleeding into reliable media as well. No, they hadn't caught any people smugglers in the last quarter. Yes, it did cost several hundreds of millions of dollars to keep it running. But you don't train a guard dog to kill intruders. You train it to keep intruders away. Why couldn't they see that there is no better indication that the money is well spent than the fact that the program appears now to be useless.

What he wouldn't give for a result though. Every time they got close, something in the ocean was vanishing their prey.

He clasped his hands together and bowed his head.

"Lord" he whispered under this breath.

"Send me heathens. Deliver me the poor and wretched so that I might protect my country and my citizens. May your divinity shine through my righteous actions."

When the radar picked up a vessel with no transponder a

few days later Captain Ian Thompson saw it as divine will. He day-dreamed about what heroic decisions he would make if they refused to be compliant. 'What would Jesus do?' he pondered. What coercive tactic would the Lord select?

The retrieval team deployed their speedboat and the helicopter gunship leapt into the air to provide emotional support.

"Bearing change 8 degrees. Speed 31 knots." read out a young ensign.

He grabbed his binoculars and scanned the choppy sea for them.

"The hell?"

A bright silver triangular sail jabbed at the sky.

"Shit!"

This was going to be some rich white button-heads playing at being sea nomads. Yoga on the decks and dream-catchers in the windows. The ocean isn't a place for this zen nonsense. The ocean is a war-zone. His strike force had reached the vessel and the radio reports cut through the bridge noise. He steeled himself to hear the bad news.

"Two passengers."

Crap.

"Unable to provide passports. Speaking a foreign language."

Oh?

"An adult male and a young boy."

The angel and the devil that sat on Thompson's shoulders did a high five. Thompson ran out of the command bridge and down to the lower deck and watched with glee as the vessel was towed in. The MH-60R Seahawk bounded about the sky like a Labrador puppy as the boat was dragged into place. It seemed that everyone was excited. The adult male stepped across into the lower gangway, his hands bound with a plastic strip. Usually the captains looked scared but this guy looked angry. They locked eyes. After a moment the scruffy pervert slipped away from his handler and rushed him. A torrent of foreign gibberish erupted from the scraggly beard. Thompson stepped forward to meet him.

"Okay Senor Epstein. That's enough out of you."

He brought his fist out and clocked the perv across the cheek knocking him out in one strike. It felt good. It felt righteous. He was also very pleased with his joke and didn't want to waste it. He called out louder this time, again refusing to pronounce the tilde.

"Take Senor Epstein into holding."

His masked soldiers dragged the unconscious form deeper into the vessel. Captain Thompson turned his attention back to the other passenger. A boy, not yet a teen, cautiously stepped across onto the boat. He looked around with a haunted visage until he saw Thompson looking at him. Suddenly the boy beamed a huge smile. He held out his hands with his palms out and a ray of sunlight lit up the gangway. This radiant child had been saved and Thompson was the saviour. This, he thought, was what Jesus would do.

'Shame he's not white' he reflected with no sense of self-awareness.

Bruised English

Machado blinked back the stars that paraded through his vision. His face ached. He opened up his eyes and nothing really got any better so he closed them again. The pain went from his shoulder all the way up to the top of his skull. He took deep breaths. The pain slowly ebbed back to just his jaw. He slowly sat up. The stars behind his eyelids became helicopters and he started to piece things together. His anger returned. The Australian Navy.

He looked about the room. Green walls. Medical? He wondered why hospitals used green and figured it was probably a 'blood thing'. Easy to spot where blood has splashed but doesn't look like a horror film. One porthole. Circle. One door. Rectangle. A smaller rectangle was contained within the door. It slid open. It slid shut. Machado suspected this wasn't a positive step.

A few minutes later the door opened. Two very rectangular gentlemen walked into the room putting Machado in mind of a toy from his childhood that required the correct shape fed through the correct hole. Their uniforms were a fusion of tactical gear and anti-concussive plate armour. Machado felt that he may not be capable of such a blast but took the compliment anyway.

The third person through the door was the captain. He recognised his fist. He wasn't sure what mistake had been made but he was hoping he could talk his way out of it. The captain spoke. The Australian accent was an ugly nasal

cartoon voice. The tone carried distain. They say that only 7%
of language is the actual words that are spoken.
Unfortunately, those seemed to be the important 7%.

"You wouldn't happen to speak Portuguese would you?"

The captain sighed and then spoke slower and louder.
Machado hated that English speakers thought this would
make them easier to understand. He also hated that he could
work out what was being asked.

"English? No. I Not English."

He didn't even know how to say he didn't speak it. His
chances of talking his way out of this just went downhill. The
captain continued on. Machado picked out a word here and
there. He thought he detected a 'Mate' being used once or
twice but suspected it wasn't being used sincerely. Machado
had no idea what was being said so he shook his head.

The captain turned to one of the rectangles to comment.
Machado recognised the one word which was internationally
recognised and begins with an 'F'. And idea struck. He
mimed pulling out his wallet and opening it. The captain
looked at him with distrust but then snapped his fingers.
Rectangle number two handed over the wallet that had been
confiscated from Machado on the sailboat. He pulled out his
ID.

"Police"

He pointed at the badge and at himself.

The captain looked closely at the badge and back at
Machado. He showed the ID to his escorts and monosyllabic
responses indicated a lack of certitude.

When he was a boy he had a classmate that had visited
Australia. He'd returned with stories of kangaroos and
barbecues and pies filled with meat instead of custard. That
was what he envisaged. This goose-stepping intimidation
was not in the picture. He had a vague sense that Australia
was a little more right-wing than some of the other world

cultures but he'd counted two U.N. violations already and he was anxious that he may learn more before this was over.

"I demand to be taken to the consulate. Consulate! Consulate!" he repeated.

The captain smiled a wry grin. He snatched back the wallet and returned a string of snide nasal gibberish. He then turned and walked out of the room followed by his polygonal escort. This time Machado managed to understand the other 93% of what was said. The consulate was a long way away and he wasn't going to see it any time soon.

He quietly said an international word that began with an "F".

Schedule 1

Christie opened the front of the machine and pulled out a salad and a coffee. She found a spot on the park's lush grassy slope and sat with her legs crossed. The tip of the Eiffel Tower poked out from behind the apartment blocks. She took a deep breath and made a point to appreciate this lovely sunny day. This vivid blue sky. Her own life. She took a sip of the coffee. Bees convened on a discarded ice lolly. She thought about heroin. About how nice it would be to take. A cloud of shame rolled over her and out of habit she checked the time of her phone. 'After 1pm. That's the best so far' she thought. Over 3 hours since she'd last thought about getting high.

It had been 34 days (fourteen hours, 2 minutes) since she'd had her last hit. That night had been… fraught. Michèle was now out of the hospital and he had immediately returned to the horse. Christie had resolved that night to stop. Just like she had every night before.

She still remembered the elation when she and Michèle first asked the machine for heroin and it had calmly opened up and provided for them. They grabbed the pack and ran giddy as school kids down the streets and alleys of Jaurès to the squat-house room they shared. There was a novelty to having it packaged. A legitimacy. Each container looked like a Chinese takeaway box. They opened them up like children on Christmas morning. A small vial. A needle. This was one of the good ones too. The fancy ones that retract after use. She'd glanced around the room and noted a pair of used needles

146

from yesterday. She'd leaned over and slipped them into her sharps container then chided herself. They were putting themselves in danger but there was no reason to put anyone else in danger. She was about to be in no frame of mind to take care of it. Best take care of it before then.

Michèle had already begun cooking. His plastic lighter hovering under his metal spoon. He put her in mind of pompous English gentleman swilling his brandy. She continued unpacking her box. A tea candle. An oil burner. A new lighter. A strip of rubber hosing. Everything she needed. The Ikea kit of narcotic self-destruction. She lit the candle and set it underneath the tiny oil burner. The heroin powder poured out into its dish and slowly began to melt. "It's good." she heard Michèle gasp but she was concentrating on her own process.

The box held another item. A small booklet. The cover stated 'Heroin is a schedule 1 opioid. It is highly addictive and should not be taken more than once in any two month period'. She held it up to Michèle and they both giggled at the notion. It was cast aside and she got down to the serious business of 'Tripping the light anaesthetic'.

The following morning she awoke groggily to the same yearning hunger she felt every morning. Michèle was gone. She strongly suspected it was not to get bakery items. She idly checked the oil burner for residue. Without even thinking about it she took a full lick of the tiny bowl. It tasted bitter and burned and she recoiled instantly feeling a pang of shame. Sitting here, in the early morning light amongst the sharps box and the blankets, the spoons and the rubber hose, she started to cry. Muffled sobs turned into a long and painful wail. Her mind showed her images of the people she missed. Opportunities squandered. A life wasted.

A door slammed and she could hear cursing coming up the stairs. She wiped the tears from her face and dashed to the bathroom where their only water was from a bucket filled on the street. Michèle bashed into the room. He held up the same booklet that had been provided in the box. She hid the clues of her trauma from him by splashing water on her face. Michèle read the booklet out loud.

"Heroin is a schedule 1 opioid. It is highly addictive and should not be taken more than once in any two month period. You have been provided a serve one day ago and will be eligible for another in 59 days. If you have an addiction we suggest a portion of methadone… This shit goes on and on."

Christie started crying again.

"What are we going to do? Duncan doesn't pay shit for anything fenced now that everything is free. How are we going to pay?"

Michèle was pacing the floor occasionally kicking at the furnishing/detritus.

"We need another face. The machine must be able to tell who we are. We just need to find someone else to get it for us."

They wandered down to the Seine where the dealers used to hang out. It was quiet but a handful of tweakers loitered around trying their best to look relaxed and casual. They were failing. Tourists stood around pointing at the usual 'point-worthy' pieces of architecture. They glanced at her out of the corner of her eye and she pulled her hood up and shrunk her head down into the plush of her jacket.

"You, uh, dealing?" asked one youth.

Michèle shook his head.

"I need a favour. You do heroin?"

"Nuh! That shit is no good."

"Great, great."

Michèle looked around nervously before continuing.

"I need you to get two serves of heroin from the machines."

"Are you serious? Those things hand out drugs?"

Michèle could see this kid's plans for the day rapidly falling into place.

"Yes, but only once per person. If you're not going to use your allocation, can you get us ours?"

"I dunno man, what's in it for me?"

"What's your flavour?"

"Uh…" the kid trailed off.

"I'm not a fucking cop! But if you want meth that machine is only going to give you one portion every two months. I can give you mine. It's a straight swap."

"Pills. MDMA."

"Deal. Meet back here in 20 minutes."

And that was how their lives played out for weeks. Swapping and collecting all the different drugs like they were playing Pokeman cards. The dealers were suffering like so many others. The money just wasn't in circulation like it once was and now their clientele was finding better product and there was no-one to intimidate out of the market. The machine's product was so pure that dealers would swap three portions of their product for one from the machine. This stuff was selling at a premium price to those who could afford it. And this was how Michèle had ended up with product that he would later refer to as "hospital grade". Christie's reaction had been less catastrophic but the evening had involved more ambulance rides than she preferring on any given day.

Michèle had stayed in his hospital bed and she'd finally walked home at dawn. She sat on her 'not entirely destroyed' futon and picked up one of the booklets that warned her far too late of the dangers of heroin. Not that she would have listened. She read the entire thing. Front to back. Recovery options. Health care contacts. On the final page, in big blue letters it said 'Your first dose of methadone'. Underneath were instructions on dosage.

There was a blister pack with a tiny sachet of liquid.

That had been 34 days ago.

The tourists in the park wandered by without a second glance. She was just another french girl eating her salad in the park. She pulled back the hood of her jacket. People said the machines could give you anything you wanted. So far as she was concerned, they were right.

Gustavo had been escorted through the labyrinthine intestines of the ship. It was like being on a spaceship. Enclosed. Steel. Grey. The carpet felt like a layer of rubber sponge under his bare feet. The tall man who had barked orders strode the corridor with a sense of self satisfaction. He was met by a young woman with fair skin and blonde hair tied back in a pony tail. She looked like she was a host on a home renovation show. The bronze badge on her shirt read 'Spencer'. When it became clear that she was being tasked with the supervision of an eleven year old boy she smiled but only with her mouth. Gustavo subconsciously noted the overhead lighting and tilted his head. With clasped hands he looked up at her through his fringe. His big brown eyes sparkling under the fluorescent tubes. Her brow furrowed. She was trying to work something out. Gustavo pulled back the charm. Nothing to work out here. Just a normal boy.

They made their way to the mess hall. A scattering of people sat around quietly munching on their late lunch.

"I don't suppose you speak any English do you kid?"

"No English" he said, with all the calmness of a card shark drawing what might be an ace or might be a three.

"Figures" she muttered as she grabbed a tray and started loading food onto it.

Once the tray was loaded, Spencer moved back the way they had come. Gustavo had hoped they might be sitting here. He wanted to get some distance from her and simply slink into the shadows. She always seemed to have one eye on him and also, there didn't appear to be any shadows on this ship. Everything was so bright. So clinical.

They walked down a corridor and up a set of stairs. She looked down at him and he tried a warm smile. Her eyebrow raised.

"Dazzling." she said sarcastically.

The room was comfortably furnished (for a boat) but obviously unused. No photos. No mess. Sheets folded on the bed. She put the tray on a table.

"Turn out your pockets"

Gustavo looked her quizzically. She sighed and started patting each of her pockets in turn then pointed at him with both hands. Gustavo feigned realisation and emptied his pockets. There was a small plastic whistle and a tiny torch attached to a small float that he carried with him everywhere since the morning he'd been knocked off the boat. There was about a teaspoon's worth of sand. Spencer took the float and flicked the torch light on and off before returning it to the desk next to the sand. She pulled out her phone and took a photo of him, then whirled her finger. Gustavo was still trying to work out whether or not to let on that he'd understood her when she let out a murmured 'For fuck's sake' then she stepped forward, grabbed him by his shoulders and span him around. A photo was taken from behind. She then pulled his shirt up at the back and took a photo. Spun him again and took a photo of his side and neck. She then lowered the phone and took a careful look at his hairline. She pushed his now shaggy hair back and took a photo of the now partially healed bruising.

"What's this bastard been doing to you?"

She looked into Gustavo's eyes and he gave them a gently haunted look.

"What's your story kid?"

He decided to up the ante.

"Spencer" he said, reading her badge.

She started, looked down at her badge and responded, 'Anne'.

"Anne" he said, before putting his palm to his chest and saying 'Gustavo'.

She felt her defences softening. Was she being conned? She measured him up. His shirt had crinkled as he'd touched it and she leaned forward and snatched out what she'd seen in the pocket. It was a piece of white card.

"… Handout Miracle Algorithm" she read.

"You're a sneaky little bastard aren't you Gus?"

"Gustavo" he said.

"Yeah, good luck with that."

She put the invitation next to the float and the sand and took a photo of all three. There was a knock at the door and a young man in a clean uniform poked his head in.

"Captain Thompson said he wants to organise a photo with the kid that he rescued from the perv in the brig."

"I'm starting to get the feeling this kid belongs in the cell next to him."

"You, uh, want me to take him down to deck 3?"

Anne Spencer stepped forward and pushed her finger into his chest.

"Just because he doesn't speak English is not a reason to describe the ship to him."

"Yes sir."

When they turned around Gustavo held the float in his hand. He closed his eyes and clicked the second setting on the torch. Both of the seaman blanched at the shocking bright beam. He grabbed the invitation (they could keep the sand) and then raced through the door and down the corridor. In his wake, the curses of two crew members who had just learned how *dazzling* he could be.

He knew where he wanted to go, but growing up on the streets of Porto had taught him that to throw off pursuers you didn't act predictably. He sprinted up two flights. Walked casually past some very important looking people who didn't even acknowledge his existence. There were no shadows. No quirky alleys. Everything was laid out in a boring grid. Every place was an equally likely hiding spot. He needed to find somewhere they'd never think to look for him.

In a flash he knew where to go. He slipped down two flights of stairs and double checked the door numbers. He could hear running footsteps and voices and so he calmly but briskly walked in the other direction. And there it was. The room he'd just escaped. He slipped inside and scanned the room for a nook. The alarms went off just as he huddled under the desk.

After twenty minutes the alarms stopped and were replaced with an alert informing crew to be on the lookout for a young boy at loose on the ship.

The Frog

Kevin Barak slowed the engine of his Protector class power boat as it pulled alongside the "Frog" that was happily sputtered through the light swell. It was another of the plague of autonomous water craft that had been found abandoned all along the US coast. He watched as deckhands delicately hooked it and dragged it up onto the swim platform. It's tiny engines whined for a moment before detecting they no longer had any resistance. It was about 4 foot long. 2 feet across. A tiny bulbous container ship. The crew speculated over the contents but Barak knew from experience they weren't getting into this thing without the key code. Drugs? Cigarettes? It could just as easily be kitchenware or computer parts. As long as they were trying to work around customs laws it was their job to stop it.

They attached their tracking device to one of the handles along the edge of the bulbous device. A lip ring for the "Frog". Adorned in its new jewellery they took a couple of photographs and then dropped it back into the sea. It bobbed for a moment then took off on its dedicated one-way journey. The tracking tag pinged its satellite which in turn pinged their boat. Now to play a very slow game of almost non-committal cat and blissfully naive mouse.

There had been thousands of these washing up on the East coast. Anyone could log into a Uruguayan website, set a pickup point and order whatever they wanted. The Frog would be filled and deployed. As easy as Amazon. But via the actual Amazon. (Barak's sense of geography was foggy on anything south of Florida)

Once these little boats had served their purpose they would be left on the beach. At high tide they'd get washed into some of the last untouched beaches in the US and make a cluster of pontoons. Like some beaver robot had started trying to dam the ocean.

After several hours the red line they were shadowing veered in towards Georgia. Just north of Savannah. That made things easier. Local authorities were alerted. Forty minutes later and the trap was set. The Frog had set up upon its pad and would be beaming out the location to its customers. Barak watched through binoculars. The day was starting to fade.

Twenty minutes later the sunset sky was pink and orange. A white van pulled up on one of the coastal roads and two teenagers jumped out and ran down the beach. They keyed in their code and the Frog opened up. There was a very sincere high five and then a dozen boxes were loaded into the van.

"Okay! GO!" said Barak into his radio.

All at once the beachside lit up in blue and red. Half a dozen vehicles locked off escape routes. A well oiled machine. Items needed to be taxed. Customs needed to be observed. Barak and his crew sailed the thick blue line and it was moments like these that put real meaning into his life.

"Apparently it's a game."

"Say again?" said Barak.

"They say it's a card game they made and had printed. Several thousand cards with, might I say, quite amateurish artwork."

"They still need to pay taxes."

"It looks like it's barely worth the paper it's printed on, and they tell me the paper was free."

Barak pinched the bridge of his nose. How many tens of

thousands of dollars worth of resources had gone into today? How many man hours? He sighed.

"Take them in and let the lawyers work it out."

"You sure? Okay. You're the boss."

Barak looked at the Frog as it wobbled back and forth in the edge of the surf. Cartoonish under a vibrant sky. He barked one more order into his radio.

"And at least do the little bastards for littering!"

Cell

Machado stared at the ceiling and tapped a-rhythmically on the wall. How long was it going to take these clowns to get their act together? The absence of clock silently ticked. At least after being held prisoner by an eleven year old for two months his quality of captor was increasing. There was a rattling on the door and Machado prepared himself for another rectangular visitor. Instead the door frame contained something distinctly Gustavo shaped.

"Gustavo! What the hell?"

The boy looked haunted.

"Machado! They think you kidnapped me. They're going to keep you locked up."

"Whoa! We're going to sort this out. Once they get a translator I'm sure we can deal with this like grown ups."

"They're not getting you a translator. They're taking us straight to a detention centre. They said we'll be there for months! We've got to get out of here."

"Where did you hear this? How did you even understand it?"

"I speak English."

Machado smirked.

"But they don't know that."

"Yeah."

"HA! You're a sly dog."

"We've got to get out of here."

"And go where?"

"Back to our boat. If we can launch at night we can sneak away. We could just untie ourselves and float until they're out of view."

Machado sat on the bed and stroked his short beard.

"No. It won't work. They've got the full might of the Australian Navy behind them. The moment they realise that we and the boat are gone they'll turn right back around and catch us in no time."

"We can out-run them."

"In a sailboat?"

"Why won't you even try?!"

Gustavo's bottom lip started to shake. He seemed to make some decision and ran out of the room.

"I'll do it without your help!" he cried over his shoulder.

"Damnit!" whispered Machado before jumping to his feet and racing out the door.

"Gustavo, wait!"

Gustavo ran down the corridor. Machado followed. A moment later he heard a call behind him. It was in English but it had a real "My goodness I'm surprised and angry" vibe to it. Machado carefully considered how much worse he would make things if he didn't immediately surrender. This was weighed against how eagerly they drew their weapons. A crack of gunfire brought a real resolution to his dilemma and he took off after Gustavo into the stairwell heading down where he ran headlong into Gustavo coming the other way.

"Up up UP!" hissed Gustavo.

There were shouts from below.

Machado turned and the pair clattered up the stairwell followed by an increasing stream of angry sailors. A moment later they burst out onto the deck and into the crisp night air. It felt strangely calm until the alarms kicked in. Yes, he could have done without the alarms. They ran down the deck, past the enormous gun mounts and the bright orange life-boats. A crack of gunfire and a ricochet had Machado grabbing Gustavo and pulling him behind one of them. He shouted back at his pursuers.

"He's just a kid for Christ's sake! Stop firing!"

They called out a response despite not understanding him and he wondered what conversation it was that they were having. There was more gunfire. 'Probably heated' he concluded. Gustavo had climbed inside the life-boat. It was a bright orange pod. He poked his head inside.

"Come out of there! We'll be trapped."

Gustavo was snapping on his seat belt and shoulder restraints.

"No we won't."

Boots were clanging down the deck. Machado jumped in and pushed the door shut until it clicked. There were twenty seats and a simple control panel. He snapped himself in just as Gustavo grabbed the release lever. Fists hammered on the shell of the pod as it slid down the launch ramp. There was a ghastly moment of acceleration as straight down became the direction of choice for the lifeboat. It dropped ten metres into the ocean before bouncing both playfully and sickeningly to the surface. The wake from the naval vessel jostled them for a few moments and then they were left in the calm bubbles as the ship got smaller and smaller.

"They'll send out their speedboats." he said peering out the wide squat windows.

He added, mostly to himself, "That's if they don't just blow us out of the water first."

A high pitched whine got his attention and Gustavo had started up the engines. The pod got underway. It was covered in lights, bright orange, and was presumably sending out a GPS beacon to the very people they were hoping to escape.

"Never let anyone ever tell you Gustavo that you're not optimistic."

There were already the bobbing lights of the speed boats weaving across the surface under the swaying lights of the stars. Machado's mind raced. What's the best way to surrender without getting shot? What non-English noises can he make that will result in the least amount of boots to the head. He reflected on his adventure to this point and wondered if this was his lowest point. Almost immediately the seas erupted and the entire boat was swallowed by an enormous beast. Machado vowed not to ask that question of himself ever again.

The Fort

Terry listened to the *clunk tap* of each of his footsteps as he stepped along the top of the shipping container. The cool of the evening gave him goosebumps. He stared out at his fields to the East and then back at his compound. Sixteen shipping containers creating a wall and his bunker right in the middle. The end of the world was looking less and less likely and that's exactly the sort of false confidence that Terry was mindful of. He'd been raised in the suburbs of Houston by a doting mother and father who lived well and died of pleasure. (Heart disease and cirrhosis respectively)

The will specified an allotment of land in Argentina where Terry's father had been raised. Terry had flown down to organise its sale, fallen in love with it and never returned to the US. As the years went by the news got worse. Wars. Pollution. Conspiracy. His farmland felt like the only safe place. Beautiful. Idyllic. Circumstances had taught him that these things can be taken from you. He started to plan. His fort was able to store years of food. It was heavily armed. He'd organised with some of the families in the area that, come the day of reckoning, Terry's fort was the go-to location.

When Argentina joined the Uruguayan collective the Combobulators came with them. Suddenly everyone had what they wanted. All the resources everyone needed were available. Terry was cautious but even he could see the benefits the machines could provide. One of the other farmers from town showed him the machine and provided him his own seed to grow one. Back on site the machine had congealed overnight and in the morning he put it to work. Some of the older farmers had retired early. 'Everything is provided for me, Terry. Why break my back ploughing fields again.' he was told.

Terry couldn't think of anything he'd rather do. He chose this life because he loved this life. At the town meeting the subject had been broached. 'The farms are lying fallow'. Terry was usually quiet on the rare occasions he would attend but this time he took the floor.

'These machines. They've changed the way we live. They might be the most amazing gift that humanity has ever received. They're a god-send. But which god sent them, and why? If these machines stop working one day, we need to be ready. Give a man a fish, and you feed him for a day...'

He'd expected debate. There was always debate at these things. The people with little power tend to wield it like a sword. This time, there was silence. Everyone's desires had being fulfilled. What if they were taken away?

The next day the fields were filled with activity. Brand new tractors with 'Jon Diore' emblazoned on the sides. Shiny boots. New fencing. Something he had said had struck a chord and the town seemed to be working with renewed vigour.

Terry had always felt like there was more preparation to be down. He never felt safe. This was the gift he'd shared with the town and now everyone was working for a better result. When he arrived in the square there was a frisson of activity. The teen boys from the farms were loading up supplies. One of them waved at him and ran over. Terry recognised Moreno's first born. Savio.

"Mr Terry. I enjoyed your speech last night very much."

"That's very kind. Thank you Savio."

"Here take this. Everyone is putting them on their

machines."

A big blue sticker was slapped into Terry's hand.

"What's this?" he asked.

But Savio had run off.

The dusk light had dimmed when Terry climbed down from his fort walls. His personal machine was blinking a message requesting more basic elements. He'd been putting it through its paces. Replacement parts. Weapons. If the machine ever stopped providing, Terry knew that at least he would be able to keep going, and he could help others. It felt good to be self-sufficient. It felt good to be part of a community.

When he asked it for seed stores it delivered but had a small note that stated the seeds could not germinate. At least the machine had a point at which it would stop playing God.

The machine was silently pulsing. Terry pulled the sticker out of his pocket, smoothed it out then peeled the wax backing from it. He slapped it on at a jaunty angle then stepped back to admire it.

'Teach a man to fish' it said in big white letters on a navy blue background.

The Belly of the Whale

It was dark. It was silent.

The neon text danced across the sky. Gustavo pulled out his torch. In the darkness of the lifeboat two baffled expressions met. The text in the sky changed.

"What's it say?" whispered Machado.

The sudden calm had them both feeling reverent.

"It says we're safe and that we need to stay quiet. There are other languages too, but I don't understand them. I suspect they say the same thing."

The text hovered in the air a few meters away. Gustavo pointed the torch around and could make out enormous shelves. Bunkbeds! There was a 'clack' behind him and he turned to see Machado leaving the vessel.

"Wait for me!" he hissed into the darkness.

The torchlight bounced around the interior of the pod making a mirrorball pattern outside. Machado stood outside the lifeboat and bounced gently on a white cushion. The whole boat was surrounded and nestled by them. Like mushrooms. A whole fairy ring hugging the boat.

"Stay!" said Machado.

The text on the walls and ceiling changed. Tenang! Xasilloon! Du Calme! Quiet! An underline was added. A second underline was added. In the silence they heard a motor. An urgent speed boat passed overhead. They were underwater. Gustavo clicked off his torch and sat back down. Machado had obviously reconsidered his exploration and rejoined him on the lifeboat. The lifeboat lights that had been so vibrant had extinguished moments after the vessel was swallowed. Whatever had rescued them, it seemed to know what it was doing. Gustavo tried to think about what sort of technology could do that. He tried to think of anything to distract him from the fact that people had shot at him. He'd run from machine gun fire. Machine guns! Adults had fired machine guns AT HIM. His blood felt cold and he started to shiver. A lump formed in his throat and his eyes stung. He wouldn't cry. He wouldn't.

There was a sensation of movement in the darkness and he felt a warmth. Machado had wrapped his jacket around him. The body heat still in it. The shivering sensation slowly subsided. He sat quietly not crying.

There were no more speedboats though there was a hum and an almost imperceptible sensation of acceleration. A few more minutes later and the lights came up. A face appeared around the walls of the vessel and began its pre-recorded speech. Gustavo carefully followed the detective out and up onto the gangway.

"Good afternoon travellers to Australia. You have been intercepted by a New Pangaea advocate vessel."

"New Pangaea? The hell is that?" muttered Machado.

Gustavo, one ear on the video, rounded on the room. Bedbunks. And then, at the front of the vessel, a Combobulator. He scurried up and placed his palm on it. The compass glowed. It was active, even here at sea.

"If you have plans to return to your country of departure or you are set on continuing to Australia your captain will be returned to the sea and you may accompany them."

"That one! Yes! Australia!" said Machado to the disembodied voice.

"No! Look! It's a Combobulator." said Gustavo.

"And anyway" he continued "Won't the Australians just

lock you up again?"

Machado paused. He'd made it clear that he didn't want to get further mixed up in all this but now he was in too deep. Surely he'd see reason.

He started gently "I would rather be in a situation that I can control. I don't know what this New Pangaea thing is and we are not at all prepared for it. I really think we should get off this thing while we still have a choice".

Gustavo blinked.

"You're kidding me? Did you listen to the video? They want to do the right thing. What about the Combobulators? What if this ship is from 'Handout Miracle Algorithm'?"

The screens cut out midway through the French version. Silence. The words 'Handout Miracle Algorithm' sat high on the wall at the front of the boat. A moment later it was replaced with the phrase 'Welcome VIP'.

The screen returned showing an empty office. A moment later an excited face burst into view.

"Hello?" he said tentatively.

He was mid-twenties and when he moved he looked light. His grin was odd but welcoming.

Gustavo hesitantly responded "Um, Hi."

"Wow! You're so young. Do you, have an invitation?"

Gustavo pulled the piece of card from his pocket. Despite the months it still felt stiff and new. A close-up image of the card reflected on the screen.

"WOW! VIP guest number 1. Also known as…"

"Gustavo" he replied.

"Gustavo! Welcome Gustavo. Thank you for accepting my invitation. You must have had quite a journey."

"Hold on, what's going on?" said Machado. His English wasn't nearly good enough to follow.

"Who's this? Your dad? He doesn't speak English?"

Gustavo scoffed, "No, This is Machado. He only speaks

Portuguese. He's…"

"Portuguese… Give me a moment."

The face on the screen looked away and seemed to pause. After a moment it became life-like again.

"Hopefully this will make things easier for you both."

A subtitle appeared underneath each screen. It reflected, in Portuguese, 'Hopefully this will make things easier for you both.'

"Wow! That was so quick!"

Gustavo's side of the conversation popped up on screen as well, like watching SMS messages.

"So Machado is not your dad?"

"He's…" Gustavo paused for a moment, "A friend."

"A friend? Well Gustavo, I am happy to extend my invitation to both you and your friend.

"I accept!" yelled Gustavo.

"No!" said Machado sternly.

"Then it's decided!" said the figure happily clapping his hands.

He continued "Let's take a look at where you are… Off the coast of Perth? Hmm. Okay it will take about 7 days under full speed to get here. Take advantage of the Combobulator. Get some rest. I'll see you in a week. Oh I can't wait."

The screen went blank.

Gustavo gently bit his lip. He slowly turned towards Machado waiting for the repercussion.

Machado has his hand on his face. He massaged his temple with his fingertips before looking pointedly at him.

"A friend?" said the detective with a half smile, "Well that's a good sign."

The screens flashed on again.

"By the way, my name is Dave. Nice to meet you both."

The screen blinked off again leaving just the ghost of the subtitles and the echo of an Australian accent.

"Give me a picture of a tailor with a jacket."

The machine glowed and clicked. Kyle removed the image and set it next to dozens of other illustrations. A man with a moustache stood next to a dressmaker's dummy. A tape measure lay around his neck like a thin scarf. He wore a burgundy jacket.

"Give me a picture of a tailor with a jacket. There is a hook in it."

The next image was nearly identical to the first but the jacket, rather than being dapperly hung from the tailor's shoulders hung from a hook on the wall. Each photo was printed on the most astounding material the world had ever known. The pigments were rendered using atomic displacement that physically altered the wavelength of the light. None of this interested Kyle.

"Give me a picture of a tailor with a jacket. There is a hook in it. It has just been pulled out of the sea."

The next photo showed the same jacket but it was crumpled up on wet sand. Upon it lay a silvery fish with a hook hanging from its mouth.

Kyle templed his fingers and pondered the pint sized machine. He'd been working in speech recognition for a decade and nothing even came close to this. This was like magic. The machine understood context and seemed to have intuition. He wasn't even sure it didn't have a sense of humour.

He'd thrown every concept from the Winograd schema at it and it hadn't missed a beat. He'd even challenged it to some of the worse gay slashfic he'd ever read.

"Bruce and Clark gazed at each other while the world fell apart around them. He gently stroked his torso's nipples."

The machine knew which 'he' was him and which 'his' was the other him. It held the concept of where the character's relationship was and even which Batman costume had the most predominant nipples in pop culture. Kyle returned the photo to the machine for recycling. That was probably too visceral an illustration for the project.

He had his research. He just needed to compile it for his boss. Not that it would do them much good. There was a connection being made to a server somewhere. The processing didn't happen locally and when the box had been contained in a faraday cage its ability to understand rapidly diminished. 'The box's ability, not the cage's' he found himself instinctively thinking. Diving into language like this can really do a number on a human brain.

Somewhere in the world lay the most exciting code that he would never see. A machine that could parse speech like a human being. He yawned and checked the time. There was probably enough time to put down a first draft before bed. Maybe even enough for a little break. He drummed his fingers on the desk before deciding, then opened up a private window and typed 'Bruce Wayne kissing Batman'.

"Ah the Internet" he mused to himself as results cascaded down the screen, "Is there anything you can't do?"

Smoke and Fish

Machado gazed out of the windows of the vessel. They were short and wide. He peered through the clear glass looking for their destination. A glassy-voiced alert repeated every few minutes that they should "Prepare to dock".

A dark cloud formed in the sky. It was a tiny thunderhead. Bulbous on top. Flat on the bottom. It billowed faster than the other clouds in the sky and grew quickly. The flat bottom stayed as still as a rock. He narrowed his eyes. There was smoke billowing out the top of an invisible chimney. No longer was he focused on the horizon. They were approaching something quickly that bent the eyes. The blue of the horizon didn't quite match the blue in front of them. The clouds duplicated themselves as they drifted across the sky and then slid into the ether.

"You've got to be kidding me."

"Where?" said Gustavo from the opposite window.

"It's huge. But it's invisible. See there, you can see the surf crashing against the base."

"It looks like it's made of mirrors."

"Not mirrors. Look at that cloud, and the one next to it."

"It's the same cloud."

The right cloud's left edge became a sharp vertical line and the remaining body of it quickly vanished like a tape-measure retracting.

"I think it's a big video screen showing us what's behind it. Lord, how would anyone ever find it if they weren't looking for it."

"I dunno. You're pretty good at finding things."

"Yeah?"

"Well you found me, and I'm pretty good at hiding."

"That's true, but you didn't make it easy."

"How *did* you find me?"

Machado grinned.

"Your emissions."

Gustavo guffawed.

"What?!"

"I looked for where the pollution was being cleaned up. I figured you'd be using a machine before anyone else did and if the particulate content dropped anywhere in the city, that's where you were."

Gustavo pondered this as the boat got closer.

"That's pretty cool. You're a pretty crafty detective."

Machado peered up at the smoke as it rose above them.

"We're a lot closer than I realised."

The boat's engine sound adjusted. Waves splashed against nothing. They passed behind what Machado realised was an artificial breakwater. The sea became smooth. The illusion was broken this close to the structure. Enormous walls rose into the sky. Easily as tall as the highest buildings in Porto. The boat turned and they were behind the breakwater. The centre of it rose back towards the main structure like a huge rocket fin. Every surface shimmered like a chameleon's scale. The boat entered a gate and made its way down the wide passageway. Enough room to cater for half a dozen of these vessels. The walls were ancient masonry. Beams of light criss-crossed and motes of dust danced in the air. A thousand candles flickered along the walls. It was dream-like.

As the vessel progressed, the decor changed. The masonry retreated and there were more vines and trees. The beams of light flickered through boughs rather than brickwork. Water cascaded down the walls. The rainforest thinned and the vegetation became sculpted. Garden beds appeared. Geometric shapes. Quaint topiary. Marble. The tunnel ended and they could see into the harbour. It was idyllic. Like a European summer town. Ice-cream shops. Bicycles. Indulgent artworks that looked like vertical hoops. A big colourful bucket for tipping water over neighbourhood children. They docked at one of the two big piers. Gustavo was almost vibrating with excitement.

The whole starboard side of the vessel made a whirring noise and opened up like a clam. They were able to walk out onto the jetty and stand on solid ground for only the second time since they left Porto. If he strained Machado could almost imagine he could still hear the surf. There was no traffic. No roads. No birds. No people.

In the quiet they could hear one of the boat screens spring to life.

"Gustavo? I'm sorry. I'm not there to meet you. Hello?"

Machado peered in at the boat screens and caught the face of 'Dave' hovering in the air.

"Are you there? I must ask you to stay on the boat. Just for a little while."

The face was illuminated by the flickering light and trill alarm. His eyes moved to the flickering light and watched for a moment before returning.

"Just uh, stay on the boat and don't umm…"

He held up a finger as if to say 'Wait just a second' as another tinny alarm joined in chorus.

"Huh" he said, and the image switched off.

Machado was left squinting his eyes and ran his fingertips through his now cultivated moustache then turned his attention to Gustavo.

"We have to stay with the boat?" he moaned.

Machado looked carefully around the idyllic little square.

"No, let's take a little look around."

Gustavo formed a tiny fist and performed a very discrete pump, then ran up the walkway.

"Wait!"

The policeman staggered after the boy to catch him up. His sea legs made the process much less graceful that he'd hoped it would be. He moved closer to the boy.

"Just... keep your wits about you, until we work out what's going on here."

"Yeah yeah yeah" said Gustavo in a tone that Machado had come to recognise as meaning 'nah'.

Machado sniffed at the air. A vague whiff of smoke. Not the scent of a campfire, but the horrible acrid tang of something awful being released into its gaseous form. Wherever that smoke had come from it seemed to have been extinguished. He looked up and saw the sky above him. On the inner side of the island's walls were hundred of balconies. Opposite those, across the harbour and the idyllic coastal town was an identical wall of balconies. Here and there, he spotted the face of some curious inhabitant. How many people lived here?

"This grass is weird."

Machado turned to find Gustavo munching away on a hot-dog.

"Where did you...?"

He whirled around and saw a hot-dog cart, an ice creamery and a bodega. Each of them combobulators. Each of them unmanned. He turned his attention to the grass that Gustavo was running his hand across and plucked some blades. They felt normal but had no smell. He rubbed them together but instead of squishing into a paste they crumbled into silvery dust and fluttered away in the breeze. Fake.

The breeze. These walls were several stories high. Where was this breeze coming from? He left Gustavo to finish his hot-dog (and, it would later be revealed, two ice-creams) and wandered back and forth through the park stopping occasionally to lift his hands in the air. Eventually he had his answer.

"The big hoops," he said returning to find Gustavo in need of the wettest of wipes, "They're fans. The breeze is fake. The grass is fake. It's like being at a theme park."

Machado put one knee down on the ground and beckoned Gustavo close to him. Gustavo let slip a little squint of suspicion.

"What?"

"Gustavo, I've spent the last several months trying to keep you safe. Trying my darnedest to keep you from making this incredibly dangerous journey. At every turn you've managed to outplay me."

Machado was impressed that Gustavo was able to conceal his smirk. He continued.

"Now that we're here. You've won. I can't stop you, but I want to you know, I still want to protect you, and I want you to look out for me too. We could both be strangers here, or we can be a team. We're going to be better off if we're a team."

Gustavo looked up into Machado's face. Was he doing his 'charm' thing? Machado couldn't quite tell.

"Deal" he said, and put out his hand.

Machado grabbed his hand and gave it one hard shake then immediately regretted it and asked a nearby machine for a moist towelette.

They wandered further along the landscaping. Ponds dotted the parkland. He could see fish chasing each other. In some areas there were sandy shallows. In others it went straight down into deep dark depths.

"Are these fake too?"

"They're tidal! Look at the barnacles." said Gustavo pointing at the rocky ornamentation.

Intermittently along the edge there were signs with an illustrated fisherman and a big red stripe though them. Someone had left a pile of trash under the foliage. His detective instincts kicked into gear. Under several of the tropical plants ran almost invisible threads. He knelt down and tugged at one that was thrumming. As he pulled he could feel a fish tugging away on the other end and in a moment it broke the surface thrashing away. He let go and the fish returned to the depths to try to make its escape.

There was an aggressive call behind him and he span around to be confronted with four youths, each of them wielding a different weapon. Baseball bat, tyre iron, switchblade, gun. Like the ninja turtles but darker. The first one let out a stream of what may have been threats but equally may have been poetry. Machado couldn't understand a word of it.

"Gustavo? You recognise this language?"

"No. I think he's angry though."

"You think?"

The lead hoodlum said something else. He couldn't have been older than sixteen though the threat of violence added a few years.

"You lads wouldn't happen to speak Portuguese would you?"

Obviously not.

"English?" asked Gustavo.

They all turned as one to the quieter of the boys who anxiously stepped forward.

"No… fish!" he said tentatively. "Our fish for us! You go!"

Gustavo translated.

Fishing in a 'no fishing' zone. It was such a small wrong-doing but it bugged Machado. It wasn't hard to do the right thing. The damned machines would give them all the fish you could ever want. Still, it wasn't his jurisdiction. Just leave them to their fish and get the hell out of here. Some subconscious part of the brain tapped on the no fishing sign. He didn't mean to, but some policeman part of him just couldn't stop himself. It wasn't a smart thing to do and that became very clear in the moments that followed.

All four of the group took a step forward and started yelling. The end of a baseball bat was shoved into Machado's chest but he shrugged it off all while carefully watching the firearm dart around like a canary with a vengeance.

"Gustavo" he said as calmly as he could, "When I say run…"

Gustavo stepped in front of the detective and put his palms up.

"Fish for you. Your fish for you. We go."

The sun reflected off a bank of windows and sparkled in his eyes. Confidently postured weapons began to droop. With a nod of his head the leader urged them on. Machado ushered Gustavo away from the pools and towards the inner wall of apartments.

"Thanks fellas. It's been a blast." muttered Machado.

This provoked an angry retort.

"We're going!" said Machado.

"Stop talking. They can't understand you. They can only read your tone."

The handgun fired into the sky and they turned and ran. In the back of his mind Machado had a number of conflicting thoughts. One was that all his training informed him that he should run in a serpentine manner to avoid being an easy target. The second was that this seemed all but impossible as his body was no longer under his control and his panic was taking him as quickly away from the danger in a straight line. The third was idly thinking about what sort of police presence the island had. The very distant fourth thought, and this was because he actively didn't want to think it, was that their predicament could have been easily avoided and it was all his fault.

They dashed into a charming alleyway that was decked out like a boutique coffee shop and shuffled though the empty tables. There were a couple of big asian guys at the other end. They ran between them before popping back out into the daylight.

"Ai!" they called out in startled unison which immediately engaged the interest of the crowd.

They were in a mall area. Pavers instead of concrete. A market strip separating the walls of apartments. Big umbrellas bespeckled the area as did café seating clusters. Everyone was looking at them. Machado span around to see the two angry alleyway bouncers. One of them was huge. The other somehow larger. His question was in an unknown tongue but the rest of his body parts were easy to parse. Machado grabbed Gustavo's hand and took off through the boutique tables and chairs.

Pride

Kelly watched and counted the Nazi flags. These Australians had always had a lot of national pride. They tended to wear it on their backs and biceps when they were attacking aboriginals. Whenever there was a big decision to be made, whenever right-minded people tried to do what was best for everyone, there was always some pocket full of muppets with a complaint. Most of Europe had amalgamated with Portugal. So many poor countries suddenly uplifted into first world lifestyles. The Australian middle-class had seen this play out from afar and decided it wasn't fair. Most of the middle-class had a sense that there was something unsavoury about the poor getting anything that they didn't already have.

The upper class already had everything they wanted and this whole miracle machine seemed like it could be a real nuisance. Many had a sense that there was something unsavoury about the middle-class getting anything that they didn't already have.

There was a brief flurry in the newspapers that boiled down to basically 'Is getting everything you've ever wanted good for our country?' to which the masses responded 'Yes please'.

No matter how much sense it made there would always be some people who would vote against their own interests. They'd already planted their flag and it didn't matter how convincing you were that they would be better off, they'd already sunk too much into their sense of self. Or they simply

179

wanted to be contrarians. They were all here today. Parading down the streets of Melbourne, calling for… well, some sort of freedom, that was for sure.

Kelly-Anne Mitchell took another photo for her news site. Long gone were the days where 'news photographer' was its own career. Now she had to rely on the AI in her phone to make something photogenic and the spell checker to make everything legible. News reporting used to be a craft. Now it was a service. Feed the beast.

A roar erupted from the crowd. She suspected they'd tipped another Combobulator over. The major capitals had filled up with these machines like they were an unstoppable virus or a new range of electric scooters for hire. The machines had been imported from the other side of the world. In the middle of the night, trucks had delivered them to prepare for the big Australian change-over. The referendum had passed with a 96% majority. We were ready to become a part of Portugal. Kelly-Anne took a few more photos of the seething mass and then made a discrete exit.

There was a ceremony at city hall. Her press ID got her access. They had several machines present for photo opportunities. The moments of creation. Soon every home in Australia (well, the Australian part of Portugal) would have a magic device. It would change the country just like it had every country it had touched.

The official unification was at midday. It was now five past. Politicians posed in front of blocks of raw elements. Journalists drank the last government paid alcohol they would ever drink. The machines could take up to half a day to activate. No one knew the mechanism through which it seemed to understand whether it was in a valid country.

Kelly sidled close to the machine to take what would be one of millions of photos worldwide of essentially the same device. It would have been a waste of her time had the golden badge not lit up there and then.

It was active. Without hesitating Kelly stepped up and asked the machine for a copy of today's newspaper. She'd been envisaging this shot for a long time. The cheesy 'hold up a newspaper' photo but this copy would be made out of woven graphene threads. Very probably there would be misspellings in the title. The machine hummed. She could hear cheers break out around the room as the people began noticing the glowing rosette.

Kelly was the first. The very first person in what was once Australia to use the Combobulator. She tugged open the door. There was no newspaper. Instead there was a single sheet. She picked it up. A test print maybe? It was a black and white photograph. The girl staring back from the image looked kind. She had dark brown skin. Clear. Flawless. The eyes looked like jewels. Dark. Sparkling. Complex. She had a slight smile that promised a pure laugh hiding not far away.

Underneath the photo, her name. Rabia Bishara. The card felt light and strong. Kelly stepped away from the machine and saw other machines opened. The same photo was withdrawn from each machine to quizzical responses.

She turned her copy over to find what seemed to be a biography.

Rabia Bishara was born in Iran where she trained in engineering. She was passionate about justice and fairness. Due to her outspoken nature and her popularity she was forced to flee the country in the dead of night leaving her friends, family and studies behind.

On the night of April 10th, two years ago, agents of the current Australian government forcibly returned her to Iran. On arrival she was removed to a secure government location where she was tortured and then killed. They insist that there is nothing illegal about what they did.

When located in Australia the Combobulator will only ever create this memorial to the love of my life. This decision is purely due to the actions of the current government.

"Oh wow" whispered Kelly under her breath. Cries of disbelief and frustration began to flutter up into the room like startled lorikeets. Kelly pushed her way out into the street and dashed down to the paper's offices. A whole country of people had just had the rug taken out from under them. If you really want to upset someone, the best thing to take from them is their hope.

Whoever had created the Combobulators had wound up every person in the country and pointed them at the current Australian government.

They insist that there is nothing illegal about what they did.

It was going to be a bloodbath.

No Man's Land

Gustavo tried to make sense of every step that he made. People jeered them and threw food. His instincts were to stop and make things right but the language barrier and the density of the angry throng gave him the sense that now was the time to run.

"Shit!" muttered Machado.

Ahead of them was a huge ornate gateway that stretched from one side of the pathway to the other. There were no gates. It was a clear open gateway and for a moment Gustavo couldn't understand the problem, but at the base of the gateway stood another pair of bouncers. Huge shoulders ready to impede their progress.

As they zipped between the arch both men gestured them through. This wasn't, it seemed, about catching them. It was about keeping them out. The street here was empty. Chunks of food landed around them. A shot rang out and they kept running. Here and there were tables and chairs scattered and fallen. Devoid of life. 100 metres away there was another gate. More figures. Machado slowed his stride much to Gustavo's relief.

His relief was short-lived. The figures were yelling at them. They slowed to a halt not ten metres from the entryway.

"Can you make out anything?"

Gustavo tried to focus what was being said. Scraps of content snuck though.

"I think it's from the Middle East."

It didn't matter. Once again context is king. Several men stepped from the gate waving pistols around. Gustavo put his palms up and beamed a brilliant smile while his brain tried to bring back the little bit of Dari that he'd absorbed. Beside him Machado had also turned his palms up in deference to the shouting and pointing.

"We're stuck in No Man's Land. Strangers trapped between two cultures."

Gustavo looked back over his shoulder. Machado was right. Most of the pistols were trained on Machado but they would blink back and forth to Gustavo.

"No no no!" said Machado.

Gustavo could hear the tension in his voice.

"We're just trying to leave."

The detective tried to mime his way out of the confrontation but did so with just a little too much gusto for these adrenalin fuelled gunmen.

In the blink of an eye the hammer fell and one of the guns fired. There was no crack of gunpowder echoing off the streets. Just a click. A flag popped out with the word 'Blam!' in a large cartoonish font.

The moment hung in the air.

Machado moved first. He grabbed the gun with his left hand and punched the guy with his right. Around him every other weapon discharged with the same charmingly kitsch cartoon effect.

Gustavo backed off. More people were flooding out the gate. This incited a thunder from behind them. He could seem a crowd forming. No Man's Land had suddenly become Too Many Man's Land. Machado grabbed at his hand and they sprinted to the centre. Both sides of the conflict seemed to have the same idea. Bats and poles and sticks jostled out the top of the mob like a very skinny puppet show.

The floor dropped out of Gustavo's world. Just a few

inches of it. Like both feet had missed a step at the same time. And suddenly he was stuck. Trapped. He looked down and his feet were gone. His legs went down to his ankles and just stopped. He could still feel them twitching in his shoes and in a moment he worked out what had happened. Around him cries went out and he could see that everyone else was in the same predicament. Their feet had slipped into the pavement. It was like the entire street surface had melted and refrozen in an instant. Occasional weapons clattered off the pavers.

A few choice words spilled out of Machado's mouth.

Whatever had happened it was definitely working in their favour. The yelling from both sides continued but slowly ebbed as the adrenalin soured. As the space became quieter Gustavo noticed another sound. Bees? He looked up and spotted a quad-copter scouting the area. The tiny drone hovered a few metres over their heads and a speaker bellowed out commands in a language he didn't recognise. It did so again in a second language, equally impenetrable.

"Hey!" yelled Machado. "HEY!"

The little drone turned to face them. Gustavo pulled his invitation out of his pocket and held it up.

"We were invited!" he called out.

"I thought I asked you," said the drone in perfect Portuguese "To wait in the boat."

A black van rolled up to the government building. It was one of many black vans doing one of many black van things. It did not have DPRK printed on the side. It didn't need to. Tan Chul-Moo watched it approach. When the wheel reached the seventh bollard he began his descent down the steps. As planned he arrived to greet the driver just as the van stopped. His day was full of these bursts of joy. Perfectly planned timing. It made him feel like an angel.

"Wet or Dry?" he asked.

Dry cargo could be stored for weeks without attention. Wet cargo would need water at least every three days. The driver stared down at his hands still gripping the steering wheel.

"P.. powder dry" he managed.

Tan Chul-Moo's eyes widened. He scanned the area. The chalk white courtyard was empty. He reached into the air, as if to pluck some invisible fruit then snapped his fingers. His colleague burst out of the guard booth and took up Chul-Moo's position at the top of the steps.

Chul-Moo then walked around the car and tugged on the door handle. It was locked. He gritted his teeth. Wasted seconds. The driver lunged over and unlocked the door.

"Sorry. Sorry sir. Sorry"

Tan Chul-Moo stood silently. Silence was his favourite weapon. When every second has value he delighted in the thrill of using so many of them to intimidate. He stepped into the passenger seat, closed the door and buckled his safety belt.

"Sorry" repeated the driver.

"Never apologise more than once. It dilutes the intent of the apology."

"sor..." began the driver before biting himself on the lip.

"Drive"

The driver pulled away from the front steps and continued further into the compound.

"Left"

Chalk white buildings slid by the window. A democratic person scurried across the road to avoid being hit. They didn't make eye contact with Tan Chul-Moo and he didn't make eye contact with them. In the government compound you got very good at seeing with your peripheral vision.

"Right"

Chul-Moo didn't often come this deep into the grounds but he knew the layout of the grounds like they're been seared into his brain. 'Speaking of which' he mused to himself as they passed the 'Wet Storage' facility.

"Where have you driven from?"

The driver gasped in shock at being addressed.

"Uh, Chak-kol"

"Chak-kol? In the mountains?"

"Yes sir. On the coast."

"In the mountains or on the coast."

"Y.. Yes sir… The coast sir."

Tan Chul-Moo loved this. The poor schlub was on the cusp of wetting himself. In the People's Republic everyone was equal, but unofficially it was nice to remind oneself that this was in no way true.

"Stop!"

The van pulled awkwardly to a stop.

"You can get out and return to your duties."

The driver wanted nothing more than this but his hands

gripped hard on the steering wheel.

"I was told, um, told to not leave the cargo until it was safely in storage, sir."

Tan Chul-Moo looked the man up and down. Perhaps he'd underestimated him.

"It is possible that anyone who knows the location of this package will need to be executed. I say to you, for the last time, you can get out and return to your…"

The door of the van had already slammed shut. 'No wasted seconds' thought Chul-Moo to himself.

He stepped out and took the driver's seat then drove a further 80 metres and into an open warehouse where he was waved in. The warehouse door rolled shut as soon as he was inside. As regulated the warehouse manager ducked under to left Chul-Moo alone. He drove down the aisles and picked a random unit to stop in front of. The rear doors of the truck clunked open at his touch and inside was a large grey box with a glowing compass rose. He sighed.

Unloading did not take long. He rolled the gurney into an unlabelled storage unit and closed the door behind him. It was dark but for the golden logo of the machine.

"I would like, a glass of Number One Alcohol"

The machine whirred and the door opened. What he was about to do was very, very illegal and thus incredibly immoral too. He took the glass and smelled it. Divine. He then returned the glass to the machine. There was a hum and a small note trailed across the surface. Recycled.

Tan Chul-Moo opened the storage container and locked it behind him. A colleague would weld it shut later in the afternoon. He climbed back into the van and returned to 'Wet Storage'. There was a large automated door at the front but Tan Chul-Moo chose the smaller red door at the side. Inside was a bare light bulb, a concrete floor and a drain. A small red button sat next to the light switch and when he pressed it, it illuminated. He pulled out his handgun and held it to his temple.

"Like an angel" he whispered.

The Tower

The top few centimetres of the unyielding stone that trapped Machado and the boy splintered and then burst into cut pebbles. They both stepped forward and out of the shallow pool of dice.

"Dave?" said Gustavo?

"You should have stayed on the boat. You shouldn't have…"

The drone hovered for a moment. Usually a human gives off several unconscious indicators that they are thinking. This device couldn't do any of those but managed to convey the sentiment all the same.

"What's important, is to get you both to safety. Please follow me."

It whirred through the air just above their heads like several hummingbirds on a mission. They followed it to the inner plaza wall where a door clicked and slid open. Gustavo hurried through after the drone. Machado turned to look at the crowds with their feet still entombed in the street pavers, then at the door that would almost definitely close behind him. Someone else was in control of his ability to leave this place and stepping through this doorway added one more barrier between the outside world and the two of them. None-the-less, this was the way he was going.

"Gustavo!" he snapped as his eyes adjusted to the room.

Gustavo froze in his footsteps.

"What?"

"Don't forget… we're a team."

Gustavo let out a deep sigh and return to Machado's side.

"I didn't realise you'd be so slow."

"'Cautious' is the word I think you're looking for."

Gustavo made cartoonishly petulant eyes and they grinned at each other.

The room was bare. Not only unfurnished, but untextured. The parallel walls ran several metres to the opposite perpendicular wall with another identical single door in it. The floor had no tiles nor carpet. It wasn't even concrete with tiny flaws and cracks. It was just… there.

"What is this? A storage area?"

The drone described a tight arc and responded.

"This area is residential."

He looked around again at the space. A futile action as there was no way he had missed anything the first time.

"That's the base model, now let's talk extras." he chuckled.

The drone hovered a moment longer.

"Was that… a joke?"

"Yes," said Machado.

More hovering.

"Okay"

"So you can speak Portuguese now?"

"Of course. How else would I grant all the requests in Portugal?"

It turned and continued towards the far wall which had a single door that did its best to add just the tiniest bit of panache. They emerged into the sunlight and yet another public square but on the far side rose a tower. The centre piece of architecture on this island. It was so black sunlight fell into it and so straight it thumbed its nose at the concept of foreshortening. If there was an architect to this structure they'd been given a brief with one word printed in big bold letters.

'LOOM!'

It felt like science fiction. Machado balked at the mix of themes. Medieval castle, Amazonian jungle, English garden, French sea-side, New York street and now Star Trek. He was getting genre whiplash. The drone wafted toward it.

"Please don't dally" it chirped.

The square was populated with a much more sparse crowd of people. The buzzing of the drone attracted attention and this caused a stirring.

Machado broke into the same light jog that most everyone would do when they were holding up a stranger at a traffic crossing. He could see the crowd gaining enthusiasm and people had started calling out to them.

"Gustavo, run."

They tore up the last several dozen metres to the tower, the drone hovering unhelpfully alongside. The was no door. No windows. Just their own darkened reflections. The crowd was drawing in and calling out to them. Wait. Not them. To the drone. To Dave. The drone ignored the crowds and turned to Machado and Gustavo and said a phrase that Machado hated to hear.

"This is not going to be pleasant but try holding your breathe."

The wall of the building where his hands pressed against it became wet and ran down his arm. Within moments he was completely covered in liquid glass. His lungs tried to pull in air but his diagram could not expand. Even if it could his mouth was covered and the glass was dynamic but unyielding. The fluid lifted and carried him through the interface of the tower. It only took a few seconds but each one of those seconds Machado was consumed in the knowledge that he was being, well… consumed.

The glass retreated and Machado and Gustavo were spat delicately onto the marble floor.

Presentation

The relief of being free again dropped Gustavo to his knees. He took deep rapid breaths and tried to focus on the patterns in the marble floor. It was cool against his palms. As his lungs calmed he studied the floor closer and saw that the marble texture was actually tiny geometric patterns. Not real marble. More illusions by the machine. The walls were all glass. The elevators were stylish. The cherrywood staircase was majestic.

Machado leapt to his feet but his knees faltered for a moment.

"Goddamned bull-..." he half muttered.

Gustavo stood up and stared at the solid glass wall. He could see people outside with their hands pressed up to shield their eyes, peering in at the two chosen ones and tapping on the glass. On instinct he raised his hand to wave but Machado gently yet firmly grabbed his arm.

The tiny quadcopter was still outside but the voice remained.

"Gentlemen, my apologies. You have arrived at a time where there are... problems yet to solve."

"Like the fire?" quipped Machado.

"Fires are easy to contain, but they are even easier to start, if one were so inclined. But I suspect this isn't the main question you have."

"What is this place?" said Gustavo.

"That's the question." said Dave's disembodied yet smiling

voice.

"Welcome… to New Pangaea."

The ceiling was bedazzled with sparkling LED lights and the south wall lit up with blueprints whizzing dynamically across it. It seemed like a castle spinning around in the 3D presentation. An internal column with three big square rings emanating out. On the west side was the breakwater where they had entered the complex. It was a huge thin corridor that shot out into the sea. At its tip was the flange of the breakwater itself. Like a big arrow pointing towards Australia. There were three other breakwaters. One from each face. From above it looked like a compass rose.

"The governments of the world have been dictated by their most selfish citizens. By the fearful. Our species has a deep seated desire to hold onto the resources we have. It's written in our selfish DNA. If we share our riches with strangers then there may not be enough for ourselves. It's easy to stay in power when you tap into that fear."

"New Pangaea is the dream of a place where everyone is welcome. Where there is always shelter, always food. You can have everything you ever wanted."

Illustrations of cafés and chocolate shops danced across the screen. It felt like an ad for timeshare. The presentation continued.

"Even the governments of the world that try to make the dream a reality are reliant on being a cog in the great machine. Here in New Pangaea we require no imports. Every day more technology can be effectively replicated with the carbon we pull out of the atmosphere. Nearly every other element can be extracted from the sea or from deep in the Earth's crust beneath us."

The video once again showed the 3D castle first spinning then zooming out to show an enormous tube running deep into the ocean floor where it suddenly bloomed into a vast root system.

"With our Combobulator technology we can pump raw materials from deep underground without the need for drills that break nor lubricant that spoil the environment. Our smart gel simply eats through the rock itself and categorises the basic building blocks of the universe."

The view zoomed into the mid point of the vertical line and broke it into dozens of colour coded lines of different widths. A key appeared and illustrated which vertical feed line contained which element. Gustavo looked up in awe and reflected on his own experience collecting elements for the machine.

"This would have been super helpful." he said under his breath.

"But none-the-less you, Gustavo, my treasured guest, collected them by hand."

A picture of Gustavo smiling and eating a hotdog flashed up on the screen. Machado looked at him with a query in his eyes. This presentation wasn't prerecorded. The whole thing was being created on the fly.

"Indeed it was this that granted you an invitation. You initially caught my eye as you were the first person to ask the Combobulator to make a second Combobulator. Then you filled the new machine with every element. That's hard to do. It really took a collector's eye."

Gustavo grinned at the compliment.

"Then I saw what you were asking the machine for. Soaps, razors, towels, medicine. Hundreds of gift boxes. Most people used the machine to grant their own wishes. You granted others."

"I wanted to pay them for their recycled goods. It felt wrong not to."

"It's that sense of justness that will make you a valuable part of New Pangaea."

Machado had been silently stewing but piped up again.

"What exactly is Pangaea?"

The presentation continued. A map of the world appeared, though it was wrong. The land masses were creeping about the sphere.

"Pangaea was the supercontinent before it broke apart into all the continents we know. You are safe here. All our guests are safe here. Most of the inhabitants here have been rescued from the dangerous journey by boat to Australia. If the Australian Government won't meet the requirements of the global community, then perhaps we can."

"It's quite small for a supercontinent" observed Machado.

"For now," said Dave "But the countries of the world are slowly breaking down their borders."

The screen changed to show a map of the world.

"Portugal now accounts for almost all of Europe. The European Union was always going to be the easy one. They didn't really have borders anyway. Chad became Africania and now consists of ninety percent of all of the African countries. The Uraguayan collective consists of the entire continent of South America plus a smattering of central American countries and islands."

"So you want to destroy all the borders?"

"I sure do. They don't really exist anyway. And once these few collectives embrace the other small countries I'll offer to accept them into New Pangaea. If they refuse, the Combobulators will be turned off. All the world will be one again."

"With you in charge?" said Machado, less a question than a statement.

The lights flickered.

"With me in service! I'm doing the right thing, which is more than I can say for the governments of the world. And who are you to question me?"

"You're in our service?" said Machado, picking at the scab. "Are you also in service of those people in the street who are ready to tear out each other's throats?"

The screen flicked off. The ceiling lights dimmed again. There was silence. When Dave spoke again it seemed to come from a long way away.

"I've been… struggling with that. I've given them everything they need. I figured that if everyone had access to whatever they wanted then there would be no more jealousy. They keep fighting each other. That's why I've been so busy. There is no police force. I didn't think I'd need one. There's hardly any drugs. There's no gun deaths. But now I have to lock them in place and force them to cast away their kitchen knives and baseball bats. Why would anyone be angry? What more can I give them?"

"That's the problem with borders, Dave. They're not just invisible lines on a globe. They're invisible lines in people's heads."

Gustavo stepped forward.

"Mr Dave, it seems to me that these people might be scared. They've never had anything to lose before. Now they have everything to lose. When you feel like that, it's easy to find someone to get angry at. Their history will always be their history. We need to find a way to help them both into the future."

A blue star appeared on the south wall and danced down towards the floor. It traced a humanoid outline and in a moment revealed the thin awkward figure of Dave. It wasn't quite video. Not quite a cartoon. Dave nodded his head slightly and smiled.

"Gustavo. I think you might be the person I've been looking for all this time. Would you help me?"

"With what?"

"You have a skill that I lack. I lack this skill to such a

degree I can only barely make it out when it happens. But you… it's like to were made to resolve conflict. I need to you talk to these people."

Machado glanced out the window at the assembled crowd.

"I don't know that's such a good idea."

"Oh not in person" said Dave.

There was a 'ping' from the elevator and the doors slid open. Inside was a helmet hanging from the ceiling and a small drone.

"Put it on Gustavo. It's for you."

Gustavo looked up at Machado who shrugged before saying "Just be careful".

He stepped into the elevator and put on the helmet. From the helmet hung a pair of gloves that he tugged onto his hands. The drone lifted into the air and hovered in front of Machado.

"Hey!" said both Gustavo and the drone. "Look at me! I'm flying."

Machado smiled as the drone orbited him like a Disney familiar.

"I can transfer your drone connection to one outside. Once you've got the hang of it you can fly down and talk to people."

"But I can't speak their language."

"Let me help you with that. Hold still for a moment. This is going to sting."

Machado looked back at the digital avatar on the wall in concern.

"Wait! What is?"

It was too late. Gustavo squealed as a hundred tiny pin-pricks erupted on his neck and scalp. His stomach lurched. That dread sensation from the middle of a blood test. Something invading his body. Wetness on the back of his neck. The sound of light. The after-images of bass. Redgreen and Yellowblue. A distinct intuition of the amount of his memory that remained. Machado made a move towards the elevators but before he'd crossed even half the gap the sensation had abated. The pain had, at least. There was still something present in his mind. A sense of a hunger being satiated.

"How do you feel Gustavo?" said Dave.

"Weird. There's something in my head."

"Say it again in Urdu?"

"I can't speak Urdu" said Gustavo in perfect Urdu.

Machado looked on in confusion.

"What did you do to him?"

The avatar of Dave had the politeness to look abashed.

"I connected him to the main computer here and embedded some other languages in his head."

"There are cables coming out of his NECK!" yelled Machado.

"It's fine." said Gustavo.

"No! It's not!"

"Are you ready?" asked Dave.

"Send me in."

"No!" said Machado, "Do not send hi…"

And then suddenly he couldn't see. That is to say, he couldn't use his eyes. He recognised the square where they had their feet stuck in the pavement. He could see it three different ways. The images bounced around in his mind and gave him a sense of sea sickness. Something… was added to him. All three images resolved. Like uncrossing his eyes. The whole island sat in his mind. A 3D space. Everything viewable at once.

It wasn't quite like real life. His eyes and inner ear knew on some level they were being tricked. The sound he could hear from the street seemed clearer. As he turned his head… no, his attention, to the crowd he could make out tight clusters of sound. Whatever he was listening to was doing some clever filtering. The cobble stones flickered with a moire pattern as they conflicted with the resolution of the display. The sunlight wasn't too bright. The shadows were not too dark.

He moved his attention. No. Some part of him moved his attention. No. Something else moved his attention. A voice in his head? Like watching a TV while someone else channel surfs.

He started to descend to where he could see the individuals still stuck in the pavement. Again, the sensation of something added to his brain. This person was Muslim. This pair were Christian. Like tinkling bells each person's religion became obvious to him. They weren't allowed to practice here. It was one of the rules. He felt the knowledge arrive in tiny packets. Enough to deal with one at a time. A sudden compulsion to make this right. He was activated. Every instinct he had to seem disarming. Each lesson he'd learned to calm people and guide them to a solution. He needed to fix this. It was his goal. His life. His... program?

He addressed the first individual. A voice that was not his boomed across the courtyard to deliver his words. Gustavo knew his name. He knew his history. It was a moment before he realised he was speaking Arabic. With all this information it was almost too easy. The anger in the man's eyes went out. He was listening. At one point he even laughed. Gustavo knew that he was good at defusing conflict but this... this was a superpower. The conversation was light and focused. A decision was made. The man stepped backwards and up from out of the pavement. He rubbed his thigh, nodded his head and waved to the cameras that sat around the courtyard before hurrying away.

Gustavo made short work of the task. The resolution of each conversation so satisfying. Each one resulting in a bloom of dopamine. With the final aggressors released, there was a moment of calmness.

"We did it!"

Several voices. All at once. Gustavo wasn't just one person. He was many. He was Andre Villeneuve, the world class physicist. He was Louisa Morellie, the designer. He was the acclaimed architect Pierre Rotriani and he was Julia Vitale, the detective who was charged with finding him. There were twelve of them. Plus Gustavo. Plus, someone else.

Work

Irena listened to the crunching gravel as she plodded down the path. She had been born in Mozirje a very long time ago and she would die here too. Soon, she suspected. But for now, she enjoyed the crunching of the gravel. When she had walked down to the farmer's market it had been powdery dry but a brief sun-shower had filled the soil with enough moisture to calm the dust.

She had a bag in each hand full of vegetables and a little cheese. Proper vegetables. Mister Horvat from next door had one of those *machines* but she'd have no truck with it. He would have once done the same walk she was doing but now he just sat on his stoop and drank. That was the problem with people today. They were lazy. Everyone wants things handed to them on a plate. No one wants to work.

These thoughts raced through her mind like racehorses nailed to a carousel. Around and around. A flock of starlings took flight and she turned to see four youths striding down the path chattering to each other. In her day young ladies who dressed like that… well, they weren't very popular. She reflected for a moment. Well, not popular with her. They'd been quite popular with some of the men. But they, she decided, didn't count. She tried to ignore them as they easily caught up to her plodding. They wouldn't greet her. No one had any manners anymore. She'd be lucky if they didn't sling her an insult. They might even steal her bags and leave her for dead amongst the crocuses. That would show Mr Forvat.

Her brow furrowed.

The teens quickly caught her up and passed her. One of the strumpets turned and gave her a big cheery smile.

"Good morning, Ma'am"

Two of the other teens gave her a friendly little wave and the last one smiled and winked at her. WINKED! Her mouth dropped open. She hadn't been winked at for a long time. The part of her that was preparing to be mugged was struggling with the part of her that once enjoyed being winked at. Her thoughts were a rollercoaster which she did not like one bit and so out of familiarity, they returned to the carousel. Where were they off to anyway? What trouble were they up to? They each wore an identical backpack and the boys had farm tools strapped to them.

"Vandals" she muttered to herself.

She should follow them, and find out what they were up to. She was in mind to alert the authorities. Or at least to complain to Mr Forvat about these reckless winking teens. But her bags were heavy. She continued slowly along the path and within a minute the youths were gone and she was alone in the countryside again.

Her thoughts turned idly to her neighbours and she had just finished a comprehensive list of all their failings when she came across the teens again. They had joined a dozen more of their ilk and were busy tearing up one of Mr Resnik's gardens. She stopped in shock. They were swinging picks and throwing big chunks of rock over the little wooden fence. The jezebel spotted her and waved her over.

Irena spluttered out "There will be hell to pay if Mr Resnik catches you."

The girl looked at her quizzically for a moment before her face brightened.

"Oh, Resnik gave us permission. He was delighted to give the go ahead."

Irena narrowed her eyes and peered through the fence palings.

"This used to be a lovely little garden." she said, almost to herself.

"Well, you'll be pleased to know that we're hoping to restore it."

Irena's eyebrows raised and her lips threatened, well, not a smile, but slightly less of a frown.

"Well, it's nice to see some people who are still willing to do some honest work for honest pay."

"Oh, we're not being paid. This is for fun."

She started to wonder if she was being taken for a ride.

"I thought most people your age just got drunk and played with your television games."

The jezebel laughed.

"It's true! We definitely did a lot of that when the Combobulators arrived. Turns out that after six weeks of that you end up feeling god awful. So everyone starts to get bored. We've got everything we ever wanted and nobody is feeling fulfilled. My friend Silva starts baking, and she starts a baking group and she can't shut up about it. She loves it."

Irena wasn't fast enough to get a word in and the young lady continued.

"Well, Dom sees this and he says he always wanted to learn to garden. He'd do ten hour shifts at the plastics plant. Well now we've got the time. He gets talking to old man Resnik and he's happy to let us have at it. He's coming down on Friday to teach us planting techniques."

Irena was shocked.

"Once those machine came I figured there wouldn't be anyone who wanted to work. It's good to see a handful of you being a shining example."

"Actually most of our friends have picked up something to do. Baking. Painting. Building."

"I find that hard to believe. Kids these days are lazy. They don't want to work."

The girl put a frown on her face. Irena felt that it didn't suit her.

The girl said, "If I gave four hundred euro a week to all the kids in town, what would you expect them to do?"

"Well, they'd just sit around and watch television I suspect."

"Is that what you'd do?"

"Heaven's no. I like to keep myself busy."

The girl smiled again and raised her eyebrows. The conversational point hung in the air. One of the carousel horses in Irena's mind kicked its heels and threatened to bolt.

"Excuse me Ma'am. We've got a bunch of wild berries and mandarinas here. Would you like some?"

It was a young blond man. His freckled face beamed and his shirt hung open in the sunshine.

The young jezebel agreed.

"Oh, yes. You must take some."

Irena stepped back.

"I can't afford any more."

"Don't be silly. It's free."

Irena balked.

"I… er… I can't. I can't carry anymore."

"Dom. Dom!"

Irena looked over and saw a pair of naked shoulders. He turned around. The winker.

"Dom can you carry…"

She turned and met Irena's wide stare.

"I'm sorry, I didn't get your name."

"Uh, Irena" she said before realising she should have said her surname instead.

"Irena! That's my name too. It's a pleasure. Dom, can you help Irena carry these extra bags back to her house."

"Can do."

He grabbed the bag of mandarinas and wild berries, then before she could stop him, grabbed her other two bags. He hefted them up, his bare pectorals barely struggling. For a moment she worried that he would take off with them. Was she being conned?

He saw the concern in her face.

"Don't worry Irena. We'll get you home safe."

He winked at her again and somewhere inside her a horse took flight and ran for the horizon.

"Do NOT send him in!"

It was too late. The Gustavo-voiced drone in front of him dropped to the floor and went silent. Machado could feel the situation being ripped away from him. He ran towards the elevator. He'd rip the damn cables out of his neck if he had to, but before he could make it the elevator doors closed. Machado slapped his hand on the glass face where he could make out Gustavo lolling and occasionally twitching inside.

He rounded on the avatar.

"Let him out! Now!"

Dave was distracted. The fake human Machado was looking at shifted from foot to foot in a cycle. After a moment it came to life again.

"My apologies Machado. Gustavo is… ascending. He is an amazing addition to New Pangaea."

"He's just a boy! And you're talking about him like he's a newly enlisted member of your startup. Let him out!"

Dave sighed, despite not needing breath, and looked at Machado in a manner that suggested utmost pity.

"He's an integral part of the island now. This is a gift. It's more than anyone could ever want."

"He's a kid! He doesn't know what he wants."

"This is beside the point. His value to the project is such that even if he didn't want to be involved, he would have to remain. It's his duty."

The elevator started to rise and Machado heard the final

trap click shut. The entire journey he'd been waiting for it to happen. Hidden on an island in the middle of the ocean. Within enormous concrete walls. Several interior walls. Entombed in a tower without doors. And now separated from each other. Gustavo trapped in an elevator with his mind trapped in a computer.

"You don't need us. Just let us go home."

"You're half right."

The floor underneath Machado split open and dropped him, 'Wile E. Coyote' style, into the basement. He banged his shoulder on the way down then landed on his bad ankle. The trap-door closed up and left him lying in the darkness. It was quiet and his attention was drawn to his bad shoulder and his worse ankle. The pain faded and then swelled several times as it parcelled out all the information it had to provide in amounts that were impossible to get bored of despite the duration.

Eventually the physical pain left and the emotional pain was able to pick up where it left off.

Gustavo was gone. He'd had one soul duty these past several months. Keep one kid safe. Billions of humans did this every day while balancing every other part of their life. And he'd failed, in the most complete way possible. Now here he was, disposed of, in the dark. His eyes began to adjust and he could make out a faint glowing green man with one leg longer than the other. The exit sign. He made his way to his feet and flicked on his pen torch. It didn't make any difference and for a moment he thought it wasn't working. The floor was black. Completely black. He could illuminate his hand but not the surface. It just absorbed everything that was thrown at it. And it was warm. Weird.

He limped to the exit sign and found dimly-lit stairs. At the top was a simple door that opened up into the sunlight. It clunked shut behind him and Machado span cursing to see that it had no external handle. Exit only. Not only did it not have a handle, it barely had any indication it was there at all. It was set in the base of one of the breeze-creating sculptures. If Machado hadn't just exited from there he'd never believe there was a door at all.

He had no idea what to do. But amongst the physical pain, the emotional pain, and lets face it, the existential pain, he was also hungry. He sought out one of the many Combobulators and saw something that he'd never seen before. The machine had his name pulsing in a warm golden light on its surface.

Machado.

He opened the device and inside, was a letter.

To Fish

The plough slid through the Earth like a shark's fin hunting for bugs and worms to bifurcate. Thomas had made the mistake of testing the sharpness of the blade and a carefully applied band-aid now clung to his finger as a visceral reminder to farm safety. It had been dangerously painless. Traditional plows needed a bullock to drag the device through the hard earth. The combobulator made blades that were both tough and sharp. It trundled ahead of him on a pair of knobbly wheels extending back to large ape hanger handlebars, clean and tidy but for a single smear of new blood.

The last of the sod flipped over and Thomas looked back upon what he had wrought. The entire back half of his lawn was now upside down. Step one completed. He asked for a glass of lemonade from the Combobulator he had next to his back door and guzzled it. An azure winged Magpie took the opportunity to take a meal of Julienned invertebrate.

A veggie garden. He'd dreamed about this all his life. Minimising the fuel needed to get food to his table. But the expense. It was just so cheap to have someone grow carrots two hundred thousand at a time and then truck them to his local supermarket. But now suddenly the tools were free. The nitrogen fertiliser could be being sucked out of the air. He could almost taste the carrots.

Of course he could have just asked the machine for carrots. It would have delivered. Cubed or fricassee. Large or small.

Heck it could give you a carrot if the shape of the King if you asked it. Thomas read the big white letters on the sticker again before returning to study a new discomfort in his hands.

They had already started growing blisters so he grabbed a pair of gloves from the machine. It was an almost religious ceremony that all amateur gardeners embraced. Decide against the inconvenience of wearing gloves until the point you are physically reminded of what gloves are for.

The plough lay on its side and Thomas grabbed the hopper he had designed and affixed it (being careful to only cut himself one more time on the nanotech blade). It was a tray that sat just under the handle bars. He clipped it on and set the whole plough down next to the recently exposed earth. There were rocks and dry dusty clods slowly drying in the Spanish sunshine. He lifted them up and put them into the hopper. Inside was the same nanotech that the Combobulator itself relied on.

The dry earth and knotted grass disappeared into the device as the blade gave a second pass through the rough stoney spoil. Within moments light moist soil dropped out of the machine and back to the earth. It was working. He knelt down and pressed the newly made soil between his fingers. If his calculations were correct this was prime growing soil. pH balanced. Nitrogen rich. Full of the snacks that a growing bacterium needs. He rubbed the soil between his fingers and smelled it before picking up more clods of earth and grass and dropping them into the hopper.

Forty minutes later the whole yard was a grand feast for the bacteria that lay starving in the second layer of earth that hadn't gone through the machine. The technology disinfected everything that went though it whether you wanted it to or not. He was glad he wasn't relying on it for yeast or seeds. Stuff that was alive, conveniently, kept growing itself. That was in fact its entire deal.

There were several other magpies now. All picking through the freshly turned soil. He had a camera trained on his garden. He retrained it on the birds and took the opportunity to do a wrap up.

"The experiment was a success. I've turned my hard packed sandy lawn into excellent growing soil that should last me years even if I wasn't doing crop rotation. Next week I'll be planting, but thanks for watching 'Teach a man to garden' and don't forget to like and subscribe."

He pulled the camera up and focused it on his Combobulator and the blue sticker with white text.

"If you have comments about how I could make this garden better, remember "If you teach a man to fish, he'll never be hungry again."

He shut the camera off and dreamed of his future crop. He wasn't just growing carrots. He was growing himself.

The Letter

Dear Mr Machado,

I apologise for the graceless way in which I ushered you from the building. Your assistance in keeping Gustavo safe in his trip to New Pangaea is greatly appreciated. He is of great value to New Pangaea and his safety is paramount. With his help we shall move into a utopian future. Human salvation is at hand.

While I appreciate your concern, that concern simply cannot be allowed to interfere with, and I say this with no hint of hyperbole, the future of mankind.

Understand that Gustavo and indeed the tower he now resides in is off limits to you. In due time you will be allowed to return to your country of origin but for now the location of New Pangaea must remain a secret. Perhaps you will even be invited to stay here. Until such a time I have provided temporary accommodation for you. Please find attached a keycard for access to your own apartment.

I would like you to consider yourself a guest here Mr Machado, but be aware, if I am forced to evict you from the complex, it is a long and damp walk home.

Machado angrily crumpled the letter in his fist and was disappointed to see it return to its original flat shape as his hand unclasped. His stomach gave a rumble so he gave his order to the machine, took a swig from the resulting bottle and trudged to his allocated flat pausing occasionally to take another mouthful of the numbing libation.

The door clicked open. Inside was a tasteful couch. A charming table with flyers and an empty basket. Big screen TV. The screen read simply 'Welcome new citizen. Please put the basket inside your new Combobulator.' Machado did so and it popped out a moment later filled with fruit and packets of nuts. The TV then switched to show a surprised image of Machado looking at a surprised image of Machado looking at a surprised image of Machado. Each iteration then looked into the corner of the room and squinted at where the camera must have been. He turned off the TV and considered covering the camera but it was small enough that he couldn't see it which meant that there were surely plenty of cameras he would easily fail to find.

The flyers gave instruction on how to access the gym or, if desired, how to request the utility room be transformed into one. Exercise. Sewing. Rock Climbing. Even Archery. (How would that work?) Simply write what you want on the outside board. The door will lock and twenty minutes later the room will be reconfigured.

Machado tossed the flyers onto the table and took his bottle of Jenny Walker out onto the balcony. From here he could see the centre ring of apartments. Each ring of buildings appeared one floor lower than the next with Dave's tower sitting obscured in the centre. A whole city state hidden from the world behind camouflage panels. Barricaded in.

He pondered the pools below. The gym. The big screen TV. The most elaborately gilded cage. A prisoner again. Trapped in the ocean. Trapped in the city. He may as well embrace the trap. So he climbed into the bottle.

It wasn't long before he passed out, fully clothed, skewed across the plush bed. As his snoring rattled the room his combobulator quietly flash his name across its exterior. He would later arise to both the horror of his first hangover in months and a card that had only a simple illustration of a small gold pineapple.

Seamless

Amivi sat in the café enjoying the easy coffee and the uneasy peace that she'd started to adjust to over the past few weeks. She'd travelled from East Timor in the hope of a better life and now here she was with everything she'd wished for. She idly watched the passers by. Idly was how she did a lot of things these days. In her old life she worked at the docks preparing and cooking fish. Now there were no fish to prepare. They weren't even allowed to fish. Hundreds of thumbs all being twiddled. No one had any purpose. The old men argued. The young men picked fights.

Across the courtyard a movement caught her eye. She didn't recognise this man. He seemed foreign. She realised that everyone was foreign here. But this man was foreign in a more foreign way. He moved in a manner that broadcast that he didn't want to be noticed. If he had been able to see himself from the outside he would have immediately tried to stop broadcasting this appearance and he would have failed quite dismally. He dressed just too inconspicuously. He gave the impression that he was actively trying not to tippy toe.

He sauntered up to the glass wall of the centre tower and it looked like he was trying to find a way in. He was not the first to have failed. There were no doors. No windows. No conveniently human sized ventilator shafts. He stepped back and stared up at the tower. It asserted itself into the sky like a middle finger. He then continued along the wall, rounded the corner and vanished out of sight. Twenty minutes later he did it again.

The third time round seemed to be enough and she watched him flop down on one of the empty shaded benches in the park-like surrounds. Curiosity got the better of her and she grabbed a pair of fresh cups of coffee from the combobulator and approached him.

"Hello" she said, in her working tongue "Do you speak English?"

At this he jolted in his seat and scanned around for danger. A traditional idiom regarding cats and curiosity tried desperately to force itself to the front of her perception. Instead she held out one of the coffees. He made no attempt to take it which she thought was quite rude.

"I don't make… Anglish very.. good" he brokenly replied.

"ah" she said defeated, before continuing on in her native tongue "Well I got you a coffee."

His eyes grew large as dinner plates and he responded.

"Oh, ah, thank you so much."

It was perfect Portuguese. He accepted the hot drink.

"Oh! Looks like I have something in common with the mysterious stranger after all."

"You're from Portugal?"

"No, I'm from East Timor, but your ancestors decided it might be a nice place to hole up."

"They did that a lot. My place of birth sometimes feels like it has a tectonic chip on its shoulder."

"Well, I imagine finally conquering Spain may relieve that, for a while."

The stranger chuckled and smiled. It was that warm, non-committal laugh that was ninety percent politeness and ten percent trying to puzzle out what was just said.

"Spain is now an enclave of Portugal. Or at least it was when I left on my voyage."

Amivi watched gears spin for a moment.

"Hello, I'm Avimi"

"Raphael… Machado" said Raphael Machado.

"How long have you been a policeman Raphael Machado?"

That put him on the back foot. In fact she had him on so many back feet he may as well have been half a millipede.

"What… makes you think I'm a policeman?"

"I've seen a lot of policemen trying not to be noticed. I used to work on the docks."

He had what he thought was a little lightbulb of inspiration illuminate.

"No! Not like that. I worked for the fish markets. So you're looking for a way in?"

She nodded at the looming monstrosity in the centre of the island and he stared up the length of it.

"I can't even find a seal."

"That's what happens when you control the firmament itself."

"Has anyone tried to break the glass?"

"Someone managed to splinter it but it healed before they could get anywhere close to putting a hole in it. You only get in if Dave lets you in."

"Dave. What's his story?"

"He started off trying to be friendly. There was a lot of 'Welcome to this' and 'let me boast about that'.

"He seems like a boaster."

"Oh yeah. There were all these info banners."

She affected the tone of the banner.

"Welcome to New Pangaea. We take our energy and resources from deep beneath the earth. The roots of our sustainable society stretch deep into the sea bed."

Raphael chuckled.

"But every week the tone shifted more passive aggressive."

"Mmm?"

This time her affected tone sounded slightly more hurt.

"New Pangaea provides a safe environment for the restoration of fish stocks. The combobulators will provide you with every type of fresh fish without needing to dip into the ecosystem that New Pangaea has worked hard to establish."

She continued in another artificial pose.

"Traditional fishing practices are unnecessary and, temporarily unauthorised."

"The tension in the advertisements rose until one night they just stopped. The banner stands just vanished. Like he didn't have the capacity to deal with it." she said.

Machado looked up at the top of the tower.

"I think he may have added that capacity."

He looked forlorn. Like the most important thing in the world was up in that tower.

"Drink your coffee Raphael. Or it'll get cold and you'll have to break it down into its molecular components and reform it exactly as it was."

Raphael took a sip of his coffee. His shoulders relaxed just a tiny bit.

"This is Utopia. Take a nice deep breath. Take several," said Amivi "There's not much else to do."

Apple

Machado's days had started to blend into each other. He would awaken with a terrible headache, wonder what he had done to deserve such an unfair predicament and then slowly recall what actions he had taken. The piles of bottles were probably an indicator of the issue. The word 'piles' should have been a give-away. He decided to finally put the bottles back into the machine so that it could recover the literal cents worth of diamond they were made from. His inner ear overruled this decision and instead insisted that he lie very still for a moment longer. It then continued to make this decision.

Tonight, he decided, he wouldn't drink. He definitely had the will power to do that. After all, he decided that yesterday, and the day before that. Deciding was easy. It was the following through on this decision that had been the impossible bit. Focussing was unpleasant so he stared at the ceiling and unfocused his eyes. Retinal floaters wandered past his field of view on their way to some popular retinal floater event at the back of his eye. Everything seemed to gently pulse. Machado tried to concentrate on quelling the sensation but it continued none-the-less which was probably for the best as this was what was transporting oxygen to his cells.

One pulsing sensation was out of sync with all the others and as he began to focus on it, there at the edge of both his perception and his eye it resolved into his name. It was glowing on the face of the Combobulator. He leapt to his feet and lunged for the door of the device before his inner ear could make a counterpoint argument. There was an envelope inside with the silhouette of an apple on it. He tore it open. Of course, it was a super material and did not tear. It merely unfolded in an annoying clever manner that Machado resented. Inside there was only another simple image. A bow and arrow. He flipped the page. Nothing. He flipped it again. The same bow and arrow. He turned it upside down and a different image appeared. One of a very similar bow and arrow but facing in the opposite direction. Gustavo was trying to get a message to him. What it entailed he could not guess. He grabbed a pen and wrote across the back of the card 'I don't understand' then fed it into the machine. A moment later the door clicked open again and the card had new information on it. The same bow but the arrow had been fired. Not for the first time did Machado consider that he may be being patronised.

Was it a riddle? If it were a rebus it was either a very simple one or a needlessly esoteric one. Had they discussed archery? His brain was in no state to process this so he decided to ask the machine for a coffee. Before he could get the words out the machine began to glow again. He yanked open the door and pulled out a piece of card. A pineapple.

Stay in place.

He squeezed his hand into a fist and imagined it was his rage, frustration and hangover being crushed and stored away for later. He then ordered a coffee from the machine and sat on his balcony and tried to process.

The messages must be coming from Gustavo. They were using his codewords. And there were times for action and times to stay quiet. Which meant that Dave was not omnipotent. He was, falling asleep? And Gustavo could reach the controls. Archery. Was Gustavo trying to come up with a plan? A palaeolithic technology probably wouldn't have much effect on the state of the art defences. But then none of the guns here would work… except the one he'd brought with him. Was he to arm everyone? Start a revolution? They all seemed to want to pick fights but in his experience it hadn't been for idealist reasons. He asked the machine for archery equipment. A familiar click and there was a flyer that he half recognised from his first day here. The utility room.

The utility room had a double doorway and a whiteboard sitting next to the door. Someone with some skill and even more time had written the temporary purpose of the room in a very legible and considered handwriting. They had done so in their own incomprehensible language. Machado peered in. The room was filled with looms and thread. Someone was teaching themself how to weave fabric but they weren't here now so Machado rubbed the label off and replaced it with a much more scrawled 'Archery'. He could barely read it himself. The doors locked and the small gold insignia he associated with the machine appeared.

He hadn't done archery since school and he'd not been great at it. Over the course of four weeks he'd graduated from barely about to hit the ground to barely able to hit the target. He wondered whether his skills with a firearm might have upped his abilities in the intervening time. They certainly hadn't helped his handwriting. He stared at the world 'Archery' where it sat on the whiteboard. Actually he hadn't done such a bad job. He stared. It was moving. Every minute it was imperceptibly refining itself. After twenty minutes it may as well have been typed. The door clicked and the compass point pulsed with a golden light.

Machado stepped into the room and his brain tried to

make sense of the enormous open space. He bobbed his head side to side like a bird and his brain started to sift though the data. It was a projection. At first blush it was a grand field with big old elm trees along the edge and straw bales in the distance. A target draped upon each straw plinth. With a shift in perspective it became clear that the room was slightly smaller than the loom room and fabric hung from the ceiling. The live image clung to the fabric like a surround movie screen. A flock of sparrows pecked at the ground before scattering into the sky. It was quite the illusion.

Several bows sat in a rack. On the left, a simple stick with twine. On the far right sat a piece of equipment that looked like it had been torn off the roof of a cable-car. The glistening thread wound back and forth through several cams. An antenna sprung from its form both top and bottom. Machado was struck by the notion that it was judging him. He picked a simple bow up from left of the middle deciding that his first attempt in years should probably be more traditional. If the hi-tech bow could sneer it would have.

He quite quickly felt overwhelmed by this bow. He needed to pull the ends close enough that the thread could latch into the little nook but no amount of strength seemed to get him close enough. There was movement in his peripheral vision and he looked up to find Robin Hood staring at him with a broad smile.

"Hail there!" Said the apparition.

"Um… hel.." Started Machado before being cut off by what was now clearly a recording.

"Seems to me that you're having trouble stringing your bow. Never fear. Like so many other tasks it's simply a trick of knowing how."

The figure continued on in a tone that insisted that it sincerely wanted to unlock Machado's resident abilities. Machado despised it. Had the creator used a team of experts to create the single most patronising instructional video of all time they'd never come even remotely close to this. Machado was learning why Gustavo was so valuable to Dave.

He strung his bow in the hope that this medieval fop would jog on.

"To notch the arrow first hold the bow in your dominant hand."

"Piss off" muttered Machado under his breath.

"Call out if you want more help." said Robin Hood and strode off behind the frustrated policeman and out of frame.

It was calm again. Machado pulled an arrow out of a barrel of dozens and tried to work out which end was which. At the less feathered end was a rubber stopper. He couldn't remove it so assumed it was part of the system. The arrow notched into the thread. He pulled it back and let fly. Several things happened. The air was filled with coloured quills from the arrow he'd loading incorrectly and even more colourful language from the policeman who'd held the bow in such a way that the string had struck his wrist. A white welt raised from the red flesh.

"Hail there friend!"

"Goddamn it!"

"Seems that you loaded your arrow in back-to-front. Don't forget to line the two similarly coloured feathers, often called the fletching with the…"

"Piss Off again!"

"Call out if you want more help."

There was a moment of stillness. Machado took a breath, then a second breath then rounded things out with a third breath. He was just about to raise the bow when…

"Hail there friend!"

"You've got to be kidding me!"

"Seems you've struck your wrist with the string. There's no shame in wearing a wrist guard especially when your level of experience is lower than…"

"GO AWAY!"

"Call out if you want more help."

Machado notched the next arrow. The stakes were high. He did not want to hear from Robin again. There was a harmonic twang and the arrow hit the fabric wall and fell to the floor. At the same time the arrow continued on into the projected image and lodged in the target. Bullseye. Machado blinked and then did something he hadn't done in a long time. He smiled. It was very small, and only on one side of his face and it only lasted for a very brief moment. It would have lasted longer but for…

"Hail there friend! Wow! Your first bullseye. Congratulations!"

Tunnel

Detective Noah Zahn flipped back and forth through picturesque scenes of the Alzette river. Even as security footage the idyllic town of Luxembourg was a romantic marvel. Less romantic were the drug smuggling crimes he was tasked with stopping. He tapped the 'next cam' button following each of the quiet pedestrians' progress starting from Port Rouge and south from there.

Lady with two dogs. Lady with two dogs. Lady with two dogs. And back to the start. Guy in hoodie. Guy in hoodie. Guy in hoodie. Fellow in Jacket. Fellow in jacket. Fellow in jacket.

Noah squished the bridge of his nose as though trying to excise the boredom. He stared at the ceiling for a moment and even this seemed more exciting.

Red shirt cyclist. Red shirt cyclist.

…

Noah tapped the buttons and frowned. He checked the timestamps. He double checked his map.

Red shirt cyclist rode into the tunnel at Rue Laurent Ménager and… didn't come out.

It had taken him two days on site to work out what had happened. He'd had to take a thermal camera and run it along the inside of the tunnel walls. All dark blue and then the unmistakeable shape of a slightly warmer hidden door. He'd returned with the taskforce and a battering ram that didn't work.

"It's Combobulator tech," said the stout sergeant "Super tough stuff."

"I don't care what it's made of, just get it open."

"I'll just wave my damn hands shall I?"

The sergeant made a dramatic gesture and the wall opened up. Everyone was silent for a moment and a helmet poked out followed by a cautious head. He looked up and saw several police officers with machine guns and a battering ram. His eyes became big ovals and his sphincter became a tiny one.

There was a sudden flurry of activity that resulted in the cyclist lying face down on the path with only minimal injury. A quick search resulted in very little money and even fewer drugs.

"Where does this tunnel lead to, son?"

"I want to see my lawyer."

There was a time when the general populace didn't quite know their legal rights and Noah missed these times. He signalled to three other officers to follow him and had the rest of the crew deal with taking 'Red Shirt' into custody.

The tunnel was a metre and a half wide and two metres high. LED lights shone down from above onto meticulously printed road markings. It was dead straight, slowly descending for easily an hour's walk before ascending again for another hour. The light at the end of the tunnel turned out to be a hub of some sort. There was a bike rack. A water cooler. A set of lockers. There were four more tunnels, each with a small sign above it. Terry. Mum. Nan. Aldi. Detective Zahn turned around to see the sign above his tunnel read 'Work'.

There was also a spiral staircase. They rushed up it and the door at the top was unlocked. Inside was a claustrophobic basement.

"What did you forget this time, Terry?" asked a seated figure.

"Okay sunshine, who the hell are you and where are the drugs?"

The figure sprang to his feet. He was barefoot in jeans and a t-shirt that on first inspection was filthy with stains but on second instead had a band logo emblazoned. If he had taken a third inspection he would have discovered both to be true.

"Dr… drugs?"

The boy grabbed a small packet and handed it carefully to Noah. He tore it open and inside was a single bottle of pills.

"What are these?"

"My thyroxine."

There was a prescription notice printed on the side of the bottle.

"Thyroid medication?! Why do you have a drug smuggling tunnel under your house?"

"Drugs? It's just to get to work."

"How did it get here?"

It seemed that this youth wasn't as versed in the law as his compatriot and a stream of nervous information spilled out.

"I used the Combobulator. It made me a device that just chewed up the ground and turned it into tunnel walls. I just wanted an easy trip to work. Once that was done I joined it up to my mate Terry so he could ride too. Then the shops, and my family."

He pointed at a map on the wall. Five dead straight tunnels all skewing off from a central point. Noah pinched the bridge of his nose again.

"So can I assume you didn't get any permits for this?"

The boy's feet tried to hide behind each other. A moment later he was lead out into the bright Luxembourg streets that turned out to actually be in Belgium and legally in Portugal.

Amivi sat enjoying her coffee and the predawn calm. She adored the eerie quiet at this time of day. The gulls had not yet started calling. The sound of the sea could just be made out. There was a twang.

There was not normally a twang.

It was the sound of an arrow being loosed. She peered upwards looking for, she supposed, an archer of some sort. It was still too dim to make out anything on the balconies.

A minute or two later a figure dressed all in black crept out into the square and tried desperately to not look like Detective Rafael Machado acting suspiciously. He crept around the corner and she followed. It wasn't even 5am and there was already something to do.

When she found him again he was looking at the central tower and then back down at the ground. He'd walk back and forth for a while like he was looking for his glasses without the benefit of having the glasses he was looking for. After several minutes of this he suddenly flailed and tried to wipe spiderweb off his face. Once the web was in his hand his face lit up. He pulled it up and at the end was an arrow. Slowly, end over end he wound the thread up until he had an arm full of a silky nest and at the end was tied a thin strand of rope. He repeated the process until he was knee deep in what looked like jute but was almost definitely carbon fibre. The end of the rope found another rope. Thicker. Like the ropes she saw on the sailboats. He tied it off on a piece of public art that looked like a big anchor which felt quite satisfying.

The rope was quite loose and Machado pushed it against the tower so that it wasn't too visible. He untied the smaller rope and hurried back to his apartment with several hundred metres of thread of rope in his arm. Amivi took her moment.

"Hello Rafael"

"Ah! Amivi. How wonderful to see you." he lied.

"Early start on the day?"

He bunched up the rope in an attempt to look like a very normal rope transport event was taking place.

"I'm so sorry. Must rush. Big day ahead. NORMAL! Big normal day ahead. Nothing out of the ordinary. Must go. Good seeing you."

He hurried away wrestling with a slowly unravelling nest of fibre as a single rubber tipped arrow dragged behind him bouncing off the ground like an attentive puppy. Amivi returned to her now cold coffee. She popped it in the machine and grabbed a fresh one then sat back and stared up into the sky to watch the detective try to rappel from his balcony to the top of the central tower.

To Scale

Machado imagined himself the pendulum under a grandfather clock. It was easy to cast this in his mind's eye as the breeze swung him from side to side. He checked the safety carabiners again mostly to have something reassuring to focus on. The carabiner sat securely in front of him while every tower and indeed the ground itself rocked backwards and forth like a very big boat. He skootched forward and moved the carabiner over the top of the knot that connected this cordage to the next. He hoped the knot tying tutorials he'd been studying were up to the task.

He could see his reflection get closer to him with each arm length he pulled. It had been weeks of work to get to this point. He'd stopped drinking. Practiced his archery. Days of rock climbing. He looking into the terrified eyes inching closer to him twice as fast as he was to the building and felt a blush of pride. He might fail, but he was doing his best. His weight pulled the slack in the rope down and he found himself close to the top edge of the building but still a good metre and a half too low. He'd been prepared for this and pulled out a belay. This allowed him to slowly scramble his way to the lip. He peered over and to his horror found no way into the building.

The last half a metre of his trip was the hardest and most disappointing. Gustavo had sent clues. Had he misread them? There was supposed to be a ventilation system here. As he rolled over the final ledge he was struck by a surge of hot air. The rooftop was square, with a low wall that Machado had just struggled over. The centre of the roof was a low dome. Just enough to move the rainwater away, and from under the lip came a constant stream of hot dry air. He made for the corner and peered under. Just enough room for a person to crawl under there and immediately get sliced into lunchmeat. Huge fast blades. No gaps. No sneaky vent. No way in. Machado stood up and contemplated the trip back but it was too much for him and he put his head in his hands. Just a moment away from the world. The giant extraction fan barely hummed but the hot air was rushing out in a dull roar. There was no sliding through. It would dice him up like a fish in a propeller.

…

a fish… in a…

…

He scanned the rope and there, a knot. He slipped it apart and one end of his exit flicked disconcertingly over the edge to the ground. He probably should have thought this through a little. He had maybe eight metres of play in the rope. He prayed it would be enough. The other end was affixed to the installation far below. He tied a carabiner to the end, lay down on his belly and whipped it into the spinning blades. It ricocheted back and forth between the blades and the underside of the dome. In a perfect world it would have sparked but there was no metal, just graphene. Finally the carabiner zipped through and quickly wrapped around the down-rod which in this case was an up-rod. The blades slowed, paused and then claimed a renewed vigour winding more and more rope like a fisherman with a marlin.

Machado looked over at the rope as it zipped against the lip of the building. Something had come loose. Before he was able to finish cursing his inability to tie a simple knot a large heavy blue anchor sprang up over the side of the building and wedged in the extractor fan blade. There was a horrible quiet as the energy that had happily been doing its thing instead began to store itself in the materials. Machado took the moment and slipped awkwardly between the static blades and into the vents below.

Alarm

Gustavo heard someone ask for Teriyaki chicken. Another voice asked for a packet of balloons. A ladle. Pants. A mousetrap. A cog 6mm across. These requests sat at the back of his minds. As soon as he registered each one it was gone. Just acknowledging their existence was enough. His minds. A shared consciousness where he could interface with a dozen of the smartest people on the island, if not the world.

Sometimes he was called upon to navigate difficult social interactions, but now everyone in the team had access to his mind, they could do the same thing. The thing that made him special, his art, had become just another resource. The voices continued. Dave was still asleep. That was all that Gustavo could determine. He kept them all locked out of his mind. Not with technology, but through the force of his distrust. The strength of his loneliness.

"Gustavo!"

It was a word unlike any he'd heard in weeks. It came via his ears.

"Gustavo!"

Gustavo tried to open his eyes but they wouldn't work so he watched the room using the cameras. Machado had made it into the central processing unit. The figures of his mind-mates hung strapped into the walls of the room. In the centre lay a small dais from which thick cables snaked upwards to connect with the huge computational abdomen of Dave that hung from the ceiling.

In that moment, when Machado was trying his absolute very best to remain quiet the alarms took the opportunity to take notice of the rising heat levels in this most sensitive of spaces. A myriad of lights flashed boot up cycles across Dave's form. Servos and hydraulics leapt into life. Dave spun around to face down the startled detective.

This was a moment that Gustavo remembered. Seeing Dave for the first time. He was impressed that Machado didn't scream like he had.

A complex machine hung from the gimbal. Dave hung forward from the machine like a carving of a mermaid on the prow of a ship. His torso bare. His legs obscured and entwined by the machinery. His face… seemed small. That is to say his face was enormous but his features sat in the centre. His cheeks stretched out. His forehead stretched up and backwards. At the edge of the skin the surface merged into cables. The mechanism moved forward and brought Dave closer. In this dim light Gustavo could see the flesh near the edge was covered in small tattoos. The compass rose from the machine. A repeating pattern. Over and over again.

"There was," said Dave "an accident. But you know what they say? Art is the ability to make accidents and to know which ones to keep."

"LET HIM GO!" cried Machado.

He pulled his revolver out and pointed it at the monstrous face.

Dave laughed into the barrel of the gun.

"Detective Machado. This is quite the surprise, and an unpleasant one at that. I won't be releasing the boy," said Dave, "He has completed us."

"You can't just kidnap people."

"Kidnap? I've embracing Gustavo into the most important work the planet has ever known. And after all who's going to stop me? You?"

Machado sank into the floor. His feet were trapped. Wires lashed out from the walls and bound him in place.

"You can't stop me. New Pangaea will rise. The world will be whole again. For Rabia."

"For Rabia."

Gustavo felt the phrase pass though thirteen minds including his own. There was so much anger. An unresolved regret. This is what he was good at. He probed Dave's mind again.

"You cannot currently access this mind"

If Gustavo had access to his knuckles he would have cracked them.

"It's time to make a friend."

He opened his virtual hands, palms up.

This tenacious detective had certainly come a long way. He was currently a problem. Dave liked solving problems. He didn't want to kill him. That didn't seem right at all. But he couldn't have him interfering either. Machado struggled in the cluster of wires that were under Dave's control.

"Detective Raphael Machado" he began in perfect Portuguese, "Your friend is one of the last pieces of my wonderful puzzle."

The detective stopped struggling and set his eyes carefully on Dave.

"You like puzzles? In a different world, maybe you'd make a good detective."

Dave smiled a tight grin.

"Are you trying to ingratiate yourself to me, detective? No, I have no interest in law enforcement. I'm more concerned with justice."

"The kind of justice that involves kidnapping young kids?"

"THE KIND OF JUSTICE THAT PUNISHES THE WICKED!!"

The lights that bespeckled the computers in the room flickered red and orange. Dave felt years of anger and regret buffet him. It had been a long time since he'd had an actual conversation. He pushed the rage back down. Once he had himself in hand again he continued.

"Were you ever chosen last for sport Detective?"

"I don't... uh..."

"When I was young we would have two pupils select who they wanted for their team. One at a time. Like a chess match but the pieces were people's sense of worth. I was always chosen last."

"Everyone says that. Everyone remembers the time they were chosen last."

"I was ALWAYS chosen last! I dedicated myself to practice. Soccer. I became very adept. It took months. And do you know what happened?"

"You were chosen last again?"

"It didn't matter that I was better than them. All that mattered was how popular I was."

"Maybe they were worried you wouldn't be very effective on the field if you were attached to the ceiling by a massive computer."

"Very amusing Detective. You have a gift for being flippant. So far as gifts go… it's not ideal. No, this situation I find myself in. Well, I was trying to connect myself to the computer. Keyboards are such a rudimentary interface. I didn't realise just how much bandwidth it would take for my brain to couple."

"Sounds awful. My favourite part of the day is when I turn off my computer."

"That is not an option for me. Do you know what the hardest problem was to solve?"

Machado jostled in his nest of wires. Dave took it to be a shrug.

"It wasn't the nanotech. It wasn't the power requirements. It wasn't networking together machines that could create themselves. It was understanding people. That's one thing that computers are still really bad at. Context. If you ask a machine for a vacuum, it doesn't know whether it should give or take away. It needs that little hint from a human brain. So I gave it access to one. Isn't that funny? I've spent my whole life trying to understand people. Their dumb jokes. Their cliques. Their desire to exclude. And now their happiness relies on my ability to understand them."

He could see the detective struggling to breathe and released his grip slightly.

"What about Gustavo? Do you think he's happy?"

Dave glanced towards the boy's listless form amongst the rest of group. Like a sports team ready for the game. And he was the star player.

"I may be smart Detective, but I have plenty of blind spots. It's only the most conceited man who thinks he can do everything. No, I've been collecting the great artists and thinkers from around the world. Luring them here to be a part of Planet Earth's finest moment."

"And what might that be?"

Dave looked into the middle distance. He could see his plan in his mind's eye.

"Reconciliation." he said.

Something in his brain felt good. Like the joy of meeting a new best friend.

"Soon almost all the countries of the world will join with the few that I have authorised to use the machines. Eventually Uruguay will have to join Portugal or the machines will fail. Then Portugal will have to join Chad. Finally, all the countries of the world will become a part of New Pangaea."

"With you in control?"

"There's no one else I trust with the job, detective."

"And those countries that don't join?"

"With the help of our friend Gustavo I suspect that the only countries I don't reign over are the ones I refuse to."

"You're refusing some countries? You don't seem the sort who wants to rule just part of the world."

Dave felt a pang of sadness. Memories of Rabia flooded his

mind.

"Justice" he said quietly under his breath.

"It's not justice to keep these people imprisoned in some cyberpunk hellscape."

"Sometimes you've got to be cruel to be kind."

"Kindness?! There's nothing kind about any of this."

"I am kind. But some people are not…"

Dave faltered. More images of Rabia. The sensation of close whispering. So many wonderful memories.

"Why should I be kind to them if they're too stupid…"

His vision started to blur. Home on the couch. Rabia hugging him. Being chosen first.

"Kindness isn't a reward for those who deserve it. It's a gift you give yourself."

He was safe. He was in control. He relaxed.

The second last thing to go through his mind was the smell of jasmine.

Shutdown

The monstrosity shuddered and twitched and its brain functions fell away. Machado was locked in place. No longer by the floor and the wires, but by the knowledge of what he had done. A waft of smoke trickled from the barrel of his revolver.

"bang" he whispered under his breath.

He cast off the remaining wires and stepped out of a puddle of what had until recently been the floor. It splashed around like printer toner. The monster had closed its eyes and let him go. He didn't know why but he wasn't about to give it a second chance. He raced to Gustavo and tried to wake him. The boy lolled his head but was otherwise unresponsive.

"Machado"

He span around. There was Dave's disembodied head hanging on the screen.

"Machado?" it said again.

He looked up at the still form hanging from the ceiling and then back at the screen in confusion.

"Machado! Can you hear me?"

Machado kept a close eye on the wires in the walls and carefully closed in on the screen.

"I can hear you. I don't know how I can hear you, but I can."

"Is? Is he dead?"

Machado's brain had been though a lot by this point and it let this question go through to the keeper.

"Whu?"

"Did you shoot Dave? Did you kill him?"

"Yes. I… Gustavo?"

"And are you free? Did I manage to let you go?"

"Yes, I'm free. The floor kind of… melted"

"I managed to get access to Dave's mind. He was so angry. So upset. But I found some memories… I'm still trapped in here but we think we can let ourselves out."

"We?"

"I've got some new friends in here. Some of them are pretty good with computers. Hang on."

There was a moment of silence and then a moment of noise. More specifically the sound of someone collapsing to the floor. Machado helped the man to his feet.

"Are you alright?"

"I… haven't used my legs in a while."

He blanched at the light.

"Or my eyes"

He was taller than Machado. And more stylish.

"I'm Pierre. I.."

He was interrupted by movement on his left.

Machado grabbed the girl before she too slid to the floor.

She blinked her eyes and looked up at Machado.

"Pierre?" she said.

"Julia." said Pierre. "It's me."

They hugged.

"It's so strange to only have my own thoughts in my head."

"What about Gustavo?" said Machado.

Pierre responded "He's the only one with Dave's access. He has to come out last."

They continued to assist the other bodies as they each gracelessly exited the virtual party. Soon it was only Gustavo remaining. Machado waited to catch him.

"Machado!"

"Gus?"

"There's a problem."

"You can do it buddy. I'm ready to catch you."

"I can release myself. That's not the issue. But Dave was sending out some sort of signal. Now there's an alert that the signal has stopped. It seems really important. Is Alex there?"

Machado turned to the crowd of very tired geniuses. One of them piped up.

"It's Alex here, Gustavo. What does the alert say?"

"It says the nanotech blueprints have desynced."

"Just get yourself out of there Gustavo." said Machado.

"Hold on" said Alex, "If those blueprints don't resync… Gustavo, the nanotech is very fragile. When it detects it's about to fail it uses its neighbour as a blueprint. This happens several times a minute and billions of times per Combobulator. But this introduces errors. Eventually the nanotech starts to mutate. I think these blueprints prevent that. They send out a master blueprint to reset any mutations. Can you search for the master blueprint."

"Okay."

Machado tapped Alex on the shoulder.

"How do you know this stuff?"

"It's kind of my thing. Why do you think he lured me here first?"

They heard Dave's post-humous voice return with Gustavo's words.

"It's gone."

"Say again?"

"His only copy was memorised. There's no software copy of the blueprint."

"Shit!"

"I don't think it would work anyway. It needs a human brain to function. Oh… The alert has changed."

"And?"

"Heartbeat signal must be restored in 22 hours."

Machado spoke up "What happens then?"

Alex turned to Machado.

"Grey Goo. The nanotech will keep recreating itself but its rules and limitations will start to vanish. Eventually it just keeps eating and eating until all that's left of planet Earth is…"

"Grey Goo? And then what do they eat? Themselves?"

"Themselves… Alex?" said Gustavo "What if we make them eat themselves?"

Alex tossed the idea around in his mind.

"We make the nanobots use each other as raw material… That could work. Yes. That should work.

Julia piped up.

"Hold on! Let's think about what we're doing here. This is world changing technology, and we're about to destroy it?"

"I just want Gustavo safe and disconnected from this abomination."

"We all care about Gustavo, Detective. He's been in our brains for weeks. But this is the promise of a post-scarcity world. No one has to work anymore."

"I didn't quit my job. Did you?"

"Well no. I don't know what I'd do without my job."

Machado rounded on the room.

"Anyone relish the thought of lying on a couch and eating grapes the rest of your life?"

"That's over-simplifying the…" began Julia before being cut off by Gus.

"I've done it."

"What?" asked Machado.

"I got the nanobots to eat themselves and change themselves into diamonds. It was pretty intuitive."

They looked around the room and nothing changed.

"There's a Combobulator in the next room. Gustavo? Can you open the door?"

The door slid open and they hurried out to find the combobulator shivering and throbbing. It looked like it would explode but then it began to sparkle and shrink. In one last pop every dark surface became a cascade of diamonds. Here and there in the pile were pebbles of gold, silver and dozens of other elements. There was a strange smell as all the released gasses mixed in the air.

"Okay, Gustavo. You did it. Let's get you out of there."

The face of Dave blinked off the screen. A moment later Gustavo slumped from his position on the wall and into the waiting arms of Machado. He pushed himself proudly upright and his tormented body gave immediate feedback as to the duration he could sustain this. Machado caught him before he hit the floor.

"Are you alright, Gustavo?"

"I… think so."

He reached back and touched the back of his neck. He could feel the texture where the wires had connected him to the machine. What he couldn't see was the pattern of tattoos that covered his skin back there. Machado guided him out into the lobby area watching him closely.

"You know, you just saved the world."

Gustavo looked up and considered this.

"Cool… I'm hungry."

Machado looked ruefully at the pile of diamonds.

"hmm" he said.

Scars

Alex Simmons reached up and touched the patterns that covered the back of his neck for what must have been the twentieth time. It unnerved him to think that the scars went all the way into his brain. He stood on the balcony of one of the many apartments that filled the inside wall of the island. From here he could look across to the top floor of the central tower and the room he'd been imprisoned in for all these months. Crowds of people formed down below. Panic was growing. There were no fields on the island. No livestock. A handful of fishing poles perhaps. Each room that had a Combobulator now had an inedible pile of diamonds. He suspected some of the refugees living here might have some stockpiles of food. When you live with scarcity it's hard to shake the feeling that it could all be taken away. Not a bad instinct in this case.

There was a click from behind him as the front door opened and in walked Gustavo, munching on some sort of energy bar. The detective followed him in and deposited a sack onto the floor of the living space.

"Was it there?" said Alex.

The detective reached into the bag, pulled out a packaged treat and lobbed it at him. It had a drab olive wrapper with 'Australian Border Force' embossed across the front, and in smaller letters the words 'ration bar'. The detective then pulled out a much more lurid object. It was about 40 centimetres tall and bright yellow. It looked like a model building from a 1960's sci-fi adventure. A thick saucer shape on top of a tall cylinder. The roof of it covered in solar panels and aerials. He felt it somehow incomplete without a model of Thunderbird 2 sitting next to it.

"Did you find the access to the roof?" asked Machado.

"There's no way up there. I suspect that Dave wanted to keep everything internal. This balcony has a view of almost half the sky. I think that's as good as we're going to get."

Machado propped the device up on a chair and hovered his finger over the 'on' button. He turned to Gustavo with a twinkle in his eye.

"Let's say G'day."

Gustavo chuckled. Machado hit the button and a bright light started pulsing on the top of the device. It was the first time Alex had seen the boy smile at all. He'd been though a lot. They all had. He touched his neck again and Machado noticed.

"So he was controlling you? He connected you to the computer?"

"Kind of. We were able to see and hear signals from the machine, and to communicate with it, and each other."

"That's some pretty sci-fi shit." he said pulling open an energy bar of his own.

"Actually I know teams who have been pretty close for years, but the problem is the connections. You don't want to just jam a bunch of wires into the back of someone's head. The nanotech allowed for self building wire connections on a microscopic scale. At that size, it doesn't matter if it's meat or metal. It's all just engineering. Once you overcome that problem, you just have the software issues to resolve."

"Well, that and the ethical concerns."

"True. That's usually a bigger hurdle. I guess I've been part of a pretty crazy science experiment."

"I suspect you could say that about anyone on Planet Earth

at this point."

They ate their "meals" in silence for a few moments. Occasionally the GPS buoy would blink.

Alex caught himself touching his neck again and wondered aloud, "How hard is it to get tattoos removed? Actually they're probably not even normal tattoos."

At this Gustavo touched himself on his neck. A look of concern flashed across his face.

Alex felt a pang of shame. His self consciousness had left him oblivious to the fact that he was only one of thirteen who had the same concerns.

"Well I think they look cool." said Machado.

Gustavo pondered this for a moment and then bobbed his head like a fifties greaser. He smiled a very slight smile again.

A moment later he asked "How long do you think it will take for someone to find us?"

Machado responded, "The Australian Border Force seem pretty well funded. I suspect we won't be waiting long."

Evacuation

It had taken only three days for the HMAS Glenelg to reach
New Pangaea. Gustavo had been on one of the first boats and
now found himself sitting in an oppressive meeting room
with Machado, Captain Tag Mitchell, a translator and the
other twelve members of what Gustavo had diligently been
trying to brand 'Dave's Thirteen'. Occasionally he had been
called on to fill in some blanks but most of the conversation
was grown-ups talking about stuff he already knew.

He stared out the window and watched the small
runabouts ferrying food over and people back. There
apparently wasn't enough room on this vessel for the
hundreds of inhabitants of New Pangaea but there were more
vessels on the way. Everyone would get rescued eventually.
Rescued from Utopia. Once again they were refugees. In a
way, so was he. This entire adventure, there had been so
much hope. A place where he belonged always on the
horizon. That hope had now been dashed. No family. No
grandfather. No home.

A lump filled his throat and he slipped down in his seat
and under the table. Here in the darkness surrounded by legs,
both table and human, tears trickled down his cheeks as he
allowed himself to feel really genuinely sorry for himself. He
closed his eyes and felt the heat of embarrassment and
disappointment wash over him.

There was a vague sense of movement and an arm reached
down holding a single tissue. He grabbed it, wiped his face

and then tried to blow his nose as discreetly as an eleven year old boy can. A face dropped down behind him.

"psst" whispered Machado.

Gustavo looked over his shoulder to see the detective conspiratorially nodding his head towards the door. He climbed out from under the table and followed him out of the room glancing back to see the rest of the group continue on with the debrief. Alex looked across at him and winked, and then they were out in the hall.

"What if they get mad?"

Machado chuckled.

"I asked if we could be done for the day. Captain Mitchell is learning that you're the big hero. He said there will be plenty of time to fill in the details and for both of us to get some rest."

"And some food?"

"Definitely!"

They strolled down to the mess and grabbed themselves some snacks. Machado ordered a beer. A small one. They sat at one of the tables and stared in silence at the setting sun.

"I'm sorry you didn't find what you were looking for."

Gustavo took a big sigh before he responded.

"When we go back how long before I don't need to live with a foster family?"

"You're only eleven, Gustavo. It's going to be a while before you can move out."

Gustavo munched on a potato chip.

"While I'm there… can I come and visit you?"

"I've been thinking about that, and I was wondering… It would be a shame to break up the team. What if you came and lived with me for a while?"

"What? Seriously?"

"Well if you don't want to…"

"No! I do. That would be awesome!"

Machado finished his beer as the sun touched the horizon. They were both lost in their own thoughts.

"You know," said Machado eventually, "When we go home, everyone else will have all this stuff the machine gave them. Everything they every wanted. I guess we ended up missing out."

Gustavo pondered his last chip.

"I think I've got everything I need already."

"Me too, pal."

The horizon ate up the very last sliver of sunset and the mess hall lights flickered on.

Gustavo looked up at Machado.

"Do you think they'll give me back my sailing boat?"

Epilogue

When the machines dissolved, many people's lives were thrown into upheaval, but not as many as you might expect. The 'Teach a Man to Fish' project had turned viral and many of the people with access to the Combobulators had used them to equip themselves with the tools to be productive in their preferred way. Home gardens were flourishing. Renovations were popular. Many had spent their time learning new skills. They just needed that initial injection of time and resources.

There was a very busy period of people suddenly realising they needed to find new jobs, but at the same time there was an enormous amount of jobs that suddenly needed to be filled. It was several months before the supply chain caught up but once it had society seemed to chug along more effectively. There had been a reset. The people who had been stuck in jobs they had grown to hate now had an opportunity to seek what that wanted. Not everyone got it, but a shuffling had resulted in a net gain for society.

Once the knowledge got out that the Combobulators would not return, Spain and France were quick to leave the Portuguese union. The other countries remained and Portugal now extended across Europe.

The African Collective consisted of every country in Africa. The decision was made to maintain this position and to rename the country 'Africa' much to the delight of geography students everywhere.

Uruguay is now massive.

The global happiness index now rates these three countries in their top twenty.

The 'trick guns' that the machine produced resulted in gun deaths in the affected countries dropping by 30%. They slowly returned to normal over the following years.

The market was flooded with cheap diamonds. The diamond cartels were ruined and diamond mines are now a thing of the past. They did try to establish a college to train people on how to tell the difference between a Combobulator created diamond and a mined one. In their attempts to reveal the organic flaws in the mined diamonds they discovered almost identical flaws in the fabricated ones. When enlarged far enough, those flaws revealed themselves to be cursive text explaining the history of blood diamond mining plus a list of names of the people who had benefited the most from this practice. The college never opened.

New Pangaea was abandoned. Without the constant upkeep by the nanobots its foundations rapidly eroded and it eventually collapsed into the sea. Only the top few floors can still be seen at low tide. The local fish population rates it five stars.

The 410 refugees from the island requested asylum. Africa, Portugal and Uraguay each accepted a share of those abandoned souls. It was, people mostly agreed, a small price to pay. Of the remaining 111 people 40 were welcomed by the United States. 35 were welcomed by Canada. 23 went to the United Kingdom. Seven to France and six to Spain.

The Australian Government promised to consider any legitimate requests for asylum.

They eventually decided on zero.

End

Jean Ngum opened the family refrigerator to find a big pot of leftover tapioca. She heaved the whole pot out and onto the bench then grabbed a bowl and a cup from the cupboard. She turned the tap and filled her cup with clear fresh water. When she was younger she remembered walking several hours to get enough muddy water for her family for the day. When the machine came it was a miracle. Her whole town became a wonderland. Plumbing, power, roads. Even a library.

Oh the library. And all the wonderful books she could read. She eagerly devoured them. No matter how much information she absorbed it felt like she'd never have too much. Indeed a thick tomb detailing bridge construction sat open on the table beckoning her return. It had been a shame when the machines stopped working. She wondered why no one had fixed them and what it would require to do that.

So much time, and nothing to do but learn.

She began to fill her bowl.

Final notes

I'd like to thank Steve Stewart for constantly engaging with every chapter as they were written. I'm not sure it would ever have been completed otherwise. Also a big thank you to Tom Seery, Jon Beeston, Steve Beeston, Jeremy Tolbert and Greg Wah for invaluable feedback.

Also thank you to my mother who fostered my love of stories and my father who fostered my love of words. All my heart to Aurelie, my first and current wife[1].

And to all the teachers who used the phrase "if he would just apply himself" in my report cards… turns out you were right.

This work was conceived and created without the use of LLMs, diffusion models, nor anything proclaiming itself to be AI, outside of the wriggly red underline of basic spellcheck and the wriggly blue one of grammar check. And my editors would suggest that those probably weren't used enough either.

If you have enjoyed this story and can get it into the hands of someone who can help lots of other people enjoy it please tell them that I can be contacted at dan@invisiblespiders.com

---

[1] Please don't tell her I described her as such so that I can maintain this arrangement.

www.ingramcontent.com/pod-product-compliance
Lightning Source LLC
Chambersburg PA
CBHW040221170726
48295CB00014B/752